The Colors of Vaud

Other works by Bryher

This January Tale

Visa for Avalon

The Coin of Carthage

The Heart to Artemis

Ruan

Gate to the Sea

Beowulf

Roman Wall

The Player's Boy

The Fourteenth of October

Bryher

The Colors of Vaud

A Helen and Kurt Wolff Book
Harcourt, Brace & World, Inc.
New York

To the memory of my parents who first took me to Vaud when I was eight

First edition

Library of Congress Catalog Card Number: 77-95857

Printed in the United States of America

Foreword

"People know about Carthage and the Battle of Hastings," my publisher said uneasily, "but whoever has heard about the Liberation of Vaud? You must begin with a brief explanation."

It is impossible to condense a rich and varied history into a couple of pages so perhaps the best beginning is to explain how I became interested in the story of my canton.

Switzerland was a magical name for me as soon as I could understand words because my father had been a mountaineer with a first ascent to his credit and long before I saw the Alps I had heard about torrents overflowing and the danger of avalanches. It was during my second visit when I was eight that we went first to Zermatt and on our return to Territet. This pattern for our summers, with the addition of the Grisons, continued until I was twelve. Naturally I did not know it at the time but I was actually sharing the last remnants of eighteenth century life because Vaud during my childhood cannot have been very different from the country I have tried to describe in this book. The children still played in the fields in the dresses of their canton, not to attract visitors but because they were the only clothes they possessed. I remember wondering how the little girls of my own age managed to do up all the buttons on their bodices and like them, I climbed up and down the hills in heavy, nailed boots.

I watched the goats scrambling up what appeared to be precipices and greeted them in the evening when they trotted down to be milked. There were no cars, no skiing, and very few roads. I drove over a pass once, feasting on small golden apricots, on top of what was almost a diligence. These coaches had ceased officially a couple of years previously but there were other passengers besides my parents and it might have been one converted to private use. I also rode triumphantly up to a mountain lake on a mule. So much that I noticed with the vivid imagination that we only possess in childhood has long disappeared but in those far off days life was still rooted in the canton's past. People then mingled very little with foreigners, each village was a realm to itself and there were many bitter feuds. Many of the changes that have taken place are for the better, there is far more freedom and less isolation but it is helpful for a student of history to have felt something of the older days happening naturally around him.

A word of warning about the present landscape. The sky, the peaks of the mountains and the lake are much the same but in the eighteenth century the vines were planted not in neat rows but dangling probably over a trellis work as they may still be seen at times in the Tessin. There were narrow bridle paths and fields between the villages that have now become towns and there are, in general, completely different flowers in the gardens. When I was free to choose the place where I wanted to live, I came back in 1921 to Vaud and apart from some years during the Second World War I have lived here ever since.

Vaud was under the control of Savoy for much of the Middle Ages although it enjoyed a certain amount of local freedom. After the Savoyards were weakened by the Burgundian wars of the fifteenth century, Berne saw an opportunity to extend its influence. It declared war on Savoy in 1536 and conquered Vaud without difficulty.

Two centuries later, the Vaudois had two objections to Bernese rule. They were the heavy taxes that they had to pay their overlords and the lack of employment for their younger sons. The peasants complained that after a bad harvest the little they had gathered had to be given up to Berne while their own families went hungry. "Leurs Excellences" also imposed rigid dates when crops might be sown or the harvest begun, regardless of weather conditions in the different regions. They were puritanical and suppressed many forms of amusement. Regulations were imposed on trading, a bad harvest could depopulate a village and there were frequent outbreaks of smallpox and plague. The babies, however, who could survive a rough and dangerous childhood, often lived surprisingly long for that period.

The second grievance concerned the growing classes of merchants, small landowners and skilled artisans. It was rare that more than one of their sons could obtain employment in his own district. They were therefore scattered across the world; there are records of them in China, Russia, India and America as well as in Holland, England and Germany. A number joined some foreign army, others became tutors or traders. A few returned home with enough savings to buy themselves a small property but the greater number died abroad or became so deeply rooted into their second country that they lived in it till they died.

A first attempt was made to free Vaud from Bernese rule in 1723 by Major Davel. It failed and he was executed.

Discontent was growing and presently revolutionary ideas began to spread across the canton from France, increasing as the refugees began to pour over the frontier after 1789. It would be a mistake to think of these fugitives as aristocrats; a few noblemen arrived but in general, they were tutors, servants or small shopkeepers who were suspect in their own country because of former connections. On the Vaudois side, the demand for freedom increased every year in spite of the Bernese who were savage in their reprisals. A number of the "patriots" as the citizens were called who were working for independence, escaped to Paris where they kept urging the French to help them attain liberty. Eventually Bonaparte—he disliked the oligarchy at Berne—gave them some support and the French government passed a decree taking the Vaudois subjects of Berne under its protection. A French army under General Ménard took up its position on the opposite side of the lake. When this was known, the Vaudois proclaimed their independence at Lausanne on January 24, 1798. Shortly afterwards, Ménard and his troops landed at Ouchy. Early in February the *"constitution helvétique"* drawn up in Paris but intended for the whole of Switzerland, reached Vaud. There were hesitations at Berne, it then called out its troops, but after heavy fighting, the city had to surrender in March, 1798.

There were still many problems to be solved but from that time Vaud became a free and independent partner within the group of cantons that we know as Switzerland.

The Colors of Vaud

Chapter One

1792

The summer storm that swept the meadows and set the peasants grumbling and shaking their heads, ceased as suddenly as it had begun. *"Bonjour,* Madame Perrin," a farmer with a rake across his shoulder and pulling a little handcart piled high with cut grass, stopped for a moment in front of a woman standing by the gate of a little house.

"Bonjour, Monsieur Gerbier, it's sad, this destruction," she pointed to the great hollows in the ripening corn, it looked as if the heavy boots of a giant army had tramped across the field, "think of the winter loaves we have lost in just over an hour."

"There is only one consolation, the less we reap, the less we pay our masters. Berne cannot tax us on what Nature has destroyed. Still I'm glad I cut this grass yesterday and left it in the shed to dry." Gerbier jerked at the cart, one of the wheels had caught against a stone, and went on at his own slow pace towards his farm.

Ces Messieurs de Berne! Think what you like about them but never mention their names, Daniel had warned his wife before they reached the frontier. Yes, their power overshadowed every act in the village, they were harsher than any father towards an unruly son because they ignored the human words, suffering, happiness or love. Madame Perrin did not like these hot, July days, they brought the past back too clearly and made her long for a cool wind off the sea. There was a difference, though friends never seemed to think of it, between people and landscapes. If she had to make her choice over again, she would still marry Daniel, even though the act had brought her from the comparative freedom of her birthplace to a spider's web of baffling rules. At home, at Hastings, it had been so easy to talk to the shy, young Vaudois who was so afraid of making mistakes in English and yet had none of a Frenchman's affectations. It had also been flattering to have him turn to her, the middle one among three sisters, the day her father had brought him back to dine. She knew that she had neither the beauty of the elder, Caroline, nor the gaiety of Sarah, the youngest of the family. "We have tempests that rise suddenly in the summer," he had told them that first evening and perhaps that was why she missed him so much during a storm, "in an hour the crops are under water and the work of the farmers ruined, sometimes for a whole year." Of course her parents had warned her about marrying a foreigner but at the time both had expected to remain in England. There were no opportunities, Daniel had explained, for a younger son in his own land. She never wanted to think again about the little house where they had spent three such happy years and where Sophie, their daughter, had been born. Yet Daniel had become strangely restless, the sea air that she found so bracing had not suited him and when a merchant had offered him the possibility of working for a time in his native country, naturally she had accompanied him. "It is only for a year or two," he had promised, "I know your Hastings, I want you to see my Lausanne."

The journey itself now seemed a patch of life that had hardly existed, full of surly innkeepers, frightened horses and often dirty rooms. All she remembered clearly was a jealous rivalry that had begun as soon as they had crossed the frontier and Daniel had shouted, "Look, my hills!" The clouds moved, the lake broke in little ripples across the sand but the mountains were still; they were nature's fortress and intimidated her, they faced her winter and summer, boys were killed on them looking for a lost goat, they were the wall that barred even the dream of an escape. She had been apprehensive from the first moment when she had seen them but she had never imagined that day that Daniel could die. Young, so young, from a fever that had lasted only a few hours.

Sarah, Caroline, a letter came from them if she were lucky, once a year. By now their dresses would be dignified gray or black but to her they were still in the gay spring skirts that they had worn that May morning on the quay. It was when the wind had caught Sarah's shawl and blown it above her ears that the parting had become real. She had watched it from the rowboat that was taking her out to the Channel ship and realized as her sister tugged at the fringes that by the time they met again, Sarah would have forgotten the incident.

A bright yellow flower, it was not a dandelion but she did not know its name, pushed its way through a crevice between the stones. If she had a few guineas (they were brighter than any flower) she could return to her own birthplace. It was a wish, would always remain a wish, because they were barely able to live on the small savings that were all that Daniel had been able to leave them and the worst seats in any diligence cost money. Yet the older she grew the more she longed for the consolation that her sisters could give her; it was "manners" here, the formal condolences murmured to any widow. The clergyman could say what he pleased, money was the only thing that mattered, a silver crown, a golden *louis,* how well she understood a highwayman risking even his life for them, they alone were the path to happiness because without them, how would either Sophie or herself get home?

"It would have been worse if the storm had come two weeks ago," the maid put a tray down carefully on the small, polished table, "think, then, of the damage to the vines."

"There are storms every summer, Marthe," Laurent Perrin put down the letter he was writing, "we have to accept what Providence sends us." Yet such tempests upset him and made him the more irritable because then they murmured in the kitchen that since his wife had died, and Dr. Tissot himself had not been able to save her, nothing that they cooked for him was right. The heavy rain would have done a lot of damage but things had to run their course. People would suffer but fate was fate. They had to accept the tempest just as they had to accept the fact that he, as the eldest son, had inherited the family vineyards and that Berne decreed their laws. Occasionally as a kind of penance he reminded himself of what it would have been like if, instead of his poor brother Daniel, he had been the second born.

The same family, the same upbringing, yet what a difference! Poor Daniel, he repeated, his brother had not profited from his opportunities. He had satisfied his employers but had neglected his own interests, he had left no debts but also few savings. His only fault had been to marry that foreigner. It was not that he, Laurent, disliked his sister-in-law, he was even sorry for her. She was a good housekeeper and deferred to his wishes but it was a responsibility and even if it had cost him a year's yield from his best farm, he would have sent her back to her own people, if it had not been for the crisis in France. Revolution! The overturning of all order and respect. And now, war! Worse, their ideas had spread like a plague. There had been that deplorable incident on the lake at Jordils the previous summer when a group of discontented fools had shouted "Down with Berne" and yelled revolutionary songs. And what had happened! A lot of the ruffians had got away but a friend of his here at Lausanne had had to walk with his fellow magistrates bareheaded through files of soldiers to express their contrition to Their Excellencies for the actions of a few drunken idiots they had never even seen.

There was no trouble here in the City. Lausanne was prosperous because its inhabitants held steadily to their good traditional ways and as if to agree with his thoughts, as people sometimes thumped their glasses on the table, Marthe knocked. "Come in, come in," he jumped up to greet his friend the notary who was coming to talk to him about the sale of a piece of land but to his amazement young Guilléron entered the room instead of his father.

"I know you are surprised to see me," the youth took the chair that Perrin indicated, "and my father sends you a thousand excuses. He is kept to his room by a severe attack of gout."

"I am sorry, very sorry," and it was not mere politeness, he liked the old notary even if he took ten sentences to explain a fact when one would have sufficed, "is he having treatment?"

"Yes, he seemed a little better this morning but it will be some days before he is able to go out."

"Well, what about this vineyard you want to sell me?"

"It is small and has been neglected but it adjoins your land."

"I know. I rode there yesterday to look at it but why does the owner want to sell? I am always suspicious if people try to get rid of fields. There is nothing safer than a solid bit of earth." The sepia dots of the seeding grasses along the verge came back into Laurent's mind. He would have dug a channel there before he planted to carry off the excess rain. "Does your father think it is a good purchase?"

"Yes and no." Guilléron was anxious to sell the vineyard

for their client but it was the first time that he had been entrusted with an important transaction and his father's final advice had been not to press Perrin. "The vines are old and the yield was poor last summer but it would round off beautifully your own bit of land."

"I am not interested in shapes." Laurent swallowed a mouthful of the expensive coffee that as he had expected old Guilléron, he had had prepared for his guest. "Besides renewing the vines would be an additional expense."

"Yet there is a risk of disease if the plot is neglected and then it could spread to your own grapes."

"What is the real reason for the sale?"

"I understand he is buying a Dutch commission for his son."

"So the family property is going to get the fool a horse."

"But there is no opening for the boy here!" Guilléron realized too late the danger of such a remark and yet how could he help making it when it was true?

"Are you presuming to question the policy of Berne?" It would be strange if the young man were tainted by revolutionary ideas after he had been brought up and trained so strictly by his father.

"Oh, no!" Guilléron fingered his papers nervously, if he irritated Perrin who was one of their best clients, he would get into trouble when he got home. "I was merely repeating what the owner of the vineyard said to us." All the same, his mind was seething, the boy had gone through school with him and now he and a dozen of his classmates were leaving, to spend their lives in a foreign land. For one who could return and buy himself a property there were three who died abroad because "the Bears" kept most of the official posts along the lake for their own sons. "We have heard this morning from a messenger who rode here from Geneva that they are frightened there that the French will attack the town." He was anxious to turn Perrin's attention away from his own unfortunate exclamation although he had meant to keep such an important item of news till the bargaining was over.

"It's those coaches full of refugees. Geneva encourages them." Nothing could be worse, in Laurent's mind, than being associated with the other end of the lake. "I am sorry for the landowners, of course, their estates have often been in their families for centuries, but why do we admit their servants? Some of them may be rebels in disguise and we don't want them spreading their revolutionary ideas here."

"Of course not, Monsieur Perrin." Guilléron ventured to drink a little coffee while it was still hot and wondered when he had had his last cup? Was it on New Year's Eve or had it been at Easter?

"Well, how much does the owner want for the land?"

"Three hundred crowns."

"Is that a joke? Remember I know the field."

"My father does not think he will go far below that price."

Guilléron looked at his saucer, even if he were offered a second cup, it would be etiquette to refuse. Sternness, that would be the word he would employ to describe Perrin, not old fashioned so much as cast in a mold that belonged to a different time, the only detail wrong was that he was not carrying a sword. "We will make him, of course, any offer you suggest but there is another would-be purchaser who came to us yesterday."

"A Dutch commission! The man is a fool. He could have placed his son in a counting house for half the money."

"It seems he has no head for figures."

"Three hundred crowns!"

"Land may be worth more than money if the French attack Geneva. It can feed us."

"Offer him two hundred and fifty. I might, I am not sure, go as far as two hundred and seventy. But not a batz more. I have too many responsibilities. My sister-in-law is a widow and besides, I have my son."

"Yes, Antoine, he is well, I hope." Actually he was an impudent little rascal, he had flung a snowball right at Guilléron's face the previous winter but his father had reminded him to ask Perrin about his family.

"Oh, you know the boy!" Laurent smiled, he was fonder of Antoine than of his vineyards or this old house in the quiet part of Lausanne that had been in his family for a century. (And looked it, some of his neighbors remarked behind his back.) "He starts at the College in the autumn."

"I watched him playing ball the other day. He is very fast for his age."

Laurent leaned over and half filled the youth's empty cup. "It won't keep till your next visit," he joked to young Guilléron's intense surprise. "Give your father my sympathy and tell him not to risk a chill by going out too soon. As for the vineyard, if the owner rejects my offer, find him another buyer. That field has been neglected for so long it would cost a lot of money to put it in order."

Twice a week Madame Perrin walked down to the market place in the center of Lausanne. She did not really need to go so often with Gerbier's farm not ten minutes from her home but its booths kept her in touch with life. Presently Sophie would be a companion but at the moment she missed her sisters so much that she felt if she turned round suddenly, she must see one of them behind her. The shouting, the bartering, the hooves, the scrunch of the wagon wheels, were easier to bear than the silence of the lonely fields. The peasant with his heavy gaiters and stick, standing in front of a row of baskets, was not unlike the laborers she had seen at home. Only his hat was different, wide and long, so that it was hard to distinguish any crown. The girls were unfamiliar with their long black mittens reaching to their elbows and twisted straw cones in the middle of their hats that reminded her of the knob on a gentleman's walking stick. She lingered here and there although she still lacked the effrontery of the village women who fingered each bolt of cloth till the trader shrieked at them to put it down, but she needed a piece of material for an apron and a remnant, if she could find one, to make Sophie a dress. The child grew out of her clothes at this age as fast as she made them. Then, according to the coins she had left, she must choose between buying a little camomile or a bunch of spices for the winter.

"A coach full of émigrés arrived this morning," a woman looked up from a great basket of berries that her children had gathered early that day on the hills. She was so plump that her skirt billowed round her in patches of brown and red, as if, to suppose it to be possible, the stuff had been dyed in a tub of apples. "Their own people attacked them and there was one poor lady in a beautiful shawl that was just a plaster of mud."

"It will teach her to do an honest day's work."

"Oh, Monsieur Édouard, have you ever done one yourself?"

Even Madame Perrin joined in the laughter because it was well known that Édouard sat in the wine shop when he should have been pruning his father's vines.

"But it's dangerous. The French are at the gates of Geneva and how do we know these are émigrés and not spies?"

"The Scriptures tell us to be compassionate."

"Not to strangers."

Madame Perrin hurried away lest some word or movement betray that she had not been born in the city. The world itself was splitting, the values of her childhood no longer existed, surely disaster must come when the young took the reins into their own hands, denied the orderly existence that she had been brought up to respect and laughed at virtues as if they were simply colored cards. It was everyone for himself and what could she or any poor fugitive do against this swelling movement that rose and flung them anywhere as haphazardly as if they were driftwood on her native beach? "I wish I were back home," the words broke involuntarily from her in a whisper but fortunately nobody heard them because a heavy coach drew up abruptly in the middle of the road. It was covered with dirt and a great scratch ran down the paint on one side. A woman in a dirty, white fichu leaned towards the window. Her companion, a serving woman from her plain, gray dress, tried to open the door but the handle had stuck. A boy, he could not have been more than thirteen, sprang down from his seat beside the coachman and tugged it ajar. "Ask them for the *Lion d'Or,* Philippe," the woman screamed, "hurry, the smell of that animal is killing me."

"They throw dead dogs at them when they get to the French frontier," a bystander muttered. "You're safe now, Madame," he shouted, a friendly grin on his face, "you're in Lausanne." The woman turned her head and did not answer him. "Proud, they are, proud but wait till they've been here a bit"; shrugging his shoulders the man walked over to a stall that was selling cakes.

"They stopped us at the Swiss frontier as well," the boy pushed his dark, rather too long hair away from his face and turned to Madame Perrin as if he felt in her some instinctive sympathy, "we were there for hours before they let us through, nobody seems to want us anywhere."

Chapter Two

An east wind blew in from the mountains and people hurried round the corner to get into the shelter of the houses. No regular patron ever shouted "Philippe" but sometimes if he was lucky there would be a cry of "Here, boy!" when a man wanted a basket carried home from the market. The other urchins clustered in the shelter of the doorways but to stand right out in the open was his single chance of getting an errand so he waited there and shivered. He had never been used to cold and dirt. There had always been enough to eat in the servants' quarters and an annual suit from Madame de Gand at the château. Then the unrest had frightened her, at a kinsman's advice she had sent her son to Utrecht to finish his education and after a house had been burned down in the neighborhood, the coach had been made ready and in uproar and confusion they had driven here from France. He had no pleasant memories of the journey, they had flung dead dogs and clods of earth at them in one village, the Swiss had threatened not to admit them when at last they reached the frontier; and a few days after their arrival at Lausanne, Madame de Gand had found she could get no more money out of France and had dismissed them. He was in rags, the wind cut through to his bare skin but perhaps because he resented pity so savagely, the other boys, in general, let him alone.

He hated this market place with its neat divisions and

grades from the big stalls full of joints and pots of cooked meat to the little stools where the poorer women sat who might have walked five miles or more to sell a single basket of greens or winter apples. He missed the sprawl and confusion of his native French village though the people here all had thick coats and laughed and shouted while the police marched about the square to see that the measures were correct and the sales orderly. They had no friends here, except for a fugitive or two as badly off as themselves; it seemed as if once they had stepped across the frontier a wall had risen between the émigrés and the universe.

A woman dragging rather than carrying a basket came round the corner. Philippe sprang forward but was just not quick enough for her to sign to him or perhaps she preferred some local boy to a foreigner? All that he had been brought up to love and respect had failed, there was no money to pay for the broth that his mother needed and he resumed his place at the windy corner next to a group of peasants, fat, chattering, sure of themselves, in the hope it was not too late for one of them to need a porter. What was the crime they were supposed to have committed? "All the émigrés bring are fleas and discontent." It might have been different if his father had been alive but he had been dead for years. Nobody could call this life if they had to exist in such misery and hunger, the word had meaning only for those who were sure of a meal, a warm room and a cloak. If it were not for his mother, he would walk down to Ouchy and fling himself into the lake.

"Madame was always good to me." Philippe had to bend over his mother to hear the words. But Madame had not been good. She ought to have left them behind, there had been a cousin in the village who would have taken them in and he could have found work there. It would have been a different life from the château, yes, but his mother would have been her own mistress. She would not have had to sit on a little stool outside the bedroom door, waiting for Madame to call her or ring the little bell that stood on a table beside her chair. He supposed he ought to be grateful to Madame for one thing, she had allowed him to sit in the schoolroom to encourage her son and although the tutor had praised his young master while appearing deliberately to neglect his companion, the man had helped him while the boy was having his riding lessons and even given him books. "These are your weapons, Philippe," he had whispered with his eyes fixed on the door, "some of us believe that rank should depend upon merit, not inheritance, so observe and seek the truth." The fool! What the fellow should have said was, "Observe and lie."

His mother was getting worse daily. It was the climate, the cold wind that blew in straight from the snows and prostrated people every autumn. More than that, it was the separation from her mistress. Madame had found she could take only one retainer with her to Holland. The coachman had been dismissed when the horses had been sold because she was joining another family in their coach but she had preferred her hairdresser, "the only person who has kept my curls compact," to the devoted service of her companion rather than maid. "I know you will find a position at once," she had assured them but Philippe doubted if she had even spoken to the innkeeper about finding them a place. Money was scarce owing to the troubles in France and who, here, wanted to employ a foreigner? The few savings they had brought with them had already been spent and his mother was getting weaker. What else could they expect in this drafty attic with a landlady who grumbled if they begged even for a jug of hot water?

Tonight his mother hardly knew him. Her mind was wandering, she thought she was walking between the lime trees in the château garden or along the corridor to Madame's room. "The chair, the one embroidered with a little girl carrying a bunch of roses, is it safe, Philippe?" He murmured "yes" to quiet her although he suspected that the notary who was supposed to protect the house had already disposed of the furniture. "Patience, and I will buy you one exactly like it," but by then his mother was murmuring about the silver candlesticks that had been used only for festivals and were her especial care. "Don't you remember, Madame brought those with her," he explained patiently but his mother either did not understand or forgot his words. Again he cursed the day when they had left their village although he had to admit that the cousin had not pressed them to remain. "All you talk about is your mistress," the man had grumbled, "and that son of yours puts on airs about reading books." What airs? Surely a revolutionary needed to read and write as much as an aristocrat if he wanted to study the speeches at the National Assembly or the opinions of his would-be leaders?

What else could he do? His mother coughed again, horribly and painfully and if the landlady heard her she might try to turn them out. "I don't want people dying in my house," she had complained already and no apothecary would give him a draught without payment. "People risk their lives to gather centaury on the mountains. They need their recompense," he had been told twice.

"I believe in the Revolution," Philippe whispered as he had done sometimes to the tutor, but if he were on its side where was the Fraternity? Why did nobody help them?

"I was in heaven and I did not know it." Philippe saw a shutter open and his mother waving to him, he could almost feel the gravel under his feet and smell the roses. It had gone but there was no reason now to linger in the market place, he was hungry, cold and could imagine no future. He knew he had ability but who wanted it in this bleak, unhelpful town? Companionship belonged to prosperity, here each was wary of the other, lest he snatch away some miserable errand that represented a day's food. He was alone, quite alone, and he knew what he had to do. Faithfulness had not saved his mother, the only gift his experiences had given him was never to believe again in virtue. Of course it was easy to be a good citizen if one had a thick winter coat. He had lice crawling over his body and a couple of youths had torn his jacket in two. No faction was just; neither Madame de Gand who had smiled at him by custom annually on New Year's Day and dragged her servants into a foreign land only to abandon them, nor the villagers who had denounced his mother for keeping to the traditions of her lifetime, nor the mobs who burned books and had howled against them at the frontier. If he had one piece of gold he would travel to the utmost land he knew, trusting no man till the end of his life, but he was not going to beg or cringe. His head was clear, he could see the future and there was one indifference greater than any human emotion. He could find it in the lake. He was no more to people than the puppy they flung in to drown. Memories, the scent of the summer roses, the tutor's whisper, "Scholarship brings its own reward," all were equally faithless but what did it matter at the end? It was only the journey that was difficult on the cold November evening, not the moment or two of struggle in the water when he reached it.

"I heard a splash," the fisherman looked down at the bundle on the floor, "I thought it was somebody tossing in a dead dog, then I heard a cry and hauled him out with my boat hook."

"Surely nobody was fishing at this time of night?"

"It's not so late, Marie, but he probably mistook that rock by the harbor for the path. It's easy enough to fall in if you don't know the way."

"Is he dead?" The woman shrank from even touching the dirty mass in front of her.

"No, he was not in long enough. Come, help me to get his coat off. Not that I'm likely to get a reward from his kin if he has any; these are not clothes, they're rags."

"The poor child."

"His ducking will have killed the fleas anyway but if that's a shirt, it's not worth drying."

"Look, Henri, it's cut in the French pattern, there, at the neck. The boy must be one of those exiles. He jumped in, he did not lose his way."

"Don't be fanciful, Marie, people say they will jump but when they see the water they start praying instead. Besides, I almost fell in myself at that very same place last year. We can spare him a corner by the fire for a day or two and I might be able to beg a jacket for him somewhere; that is, if he lives."

"He's starved," the rags came away in strips as Marie tugged at them and in spite of herself she thought sadly of the floor that she had swept and sanded only that afternoon in preparation for Sunday; the water was dribbling as far as the hearth, "he's not alive," she touched the wet body and shrieked.

"He's breathing all right," Henri pressed his hand on the boy's chest, "look, he's opening his eyes." Yet Philippe's mind was elsewhere, he was muttering words that made no sense to them, even when Marie bundled him up in her own quilt and built up the fire to a blaze that showed the cobwebs just out of reach of her broom and the damp crack in the ceiling near the door.

"What is your name?"

"Philippe Masson." He was tired of answering these questions over and over again, nobody had helped him or was likely to help him.

"You are French, they tell me."

"Yes, sir."

"Have you been in Lausanne long?"

"Since last May. My mother belonged to the household of Madame de Gand and naturally accompanied her when she had to leave her home. My father has been dead some years." How could the love and terror and deprivation he had known be put into a few, flat syllables?

"I am told that you wandered away after your mother's funeral and jumped into the lake. Surely you have listened to the Scriptures even if you cannot read them. You must have heard the preacher tell us that we must bear our sorrows with resignation."

"I can read." The man was as severe and cold as the suit that he was wearing was thick and warm and Philippe wondered if he had ever shown affection towards anyone in his life? "Besides, sir, I did not jump in on purpose," to tell the truth would only mean a beating, "I had a fever and was told of an apothecary at Ouchy who sometimes gave the suffering a *tisane* out of kindness. I fell into the lake by accident in the dark."

"It is true that your rescuer says you are a stranger and had lost your way." It had been the boatman's wife who had screamed that the child had been abandoned and had sprung in from despair. He looked at the boy sternly and Philippe kept his eyes fixed on the silver buckles of the man's shoes.

If he were alive, and it appeared he was, perhaps after so much questioning he would be offered work.

"You say you can read?"

"Yes, sir, and write as well. Madame de Gand allowed me to share the lessons of her son. She had promised to bind me to a notary," Philippe invented wildly on the spur of the moment, "I had hoped to become a clerk."

"It was the decadence in France that led to the Revolution. Still, you have lost your parents and are too young to have been poisoned by their lawless ideas. If I thought you had thrown yourself into the lake of your own will, whipping would have been too mild a punishment but Monsieur Bosset here says the path was dark and you were ill, so I accept your assurance that it happened by chance."

"Thank you, sir." How stupid people were and harsh! Couldn't his questioner realize that even now the only thing between him and the lake again was an offer of employment?

"My name is Perrin, Monsieur Laurent Perrin, and if a boy in need is diligent, I am ready to help him. First you must go to church and give thanks for being rescued. Then you can come to my house tomorrow at nine o'clock. Bosset will tell you where it is and I will ask my housekeeper to find you some clothes and a corner where you can sleep. I will give you a letter to Monsieur Guilléron. He was asking me the other day if I knew of a boy who could sweep out his office and run errands for him. I need not advise you to be obedient, you have seen for yourself what suffering it brings if the established order of any country is upset."

Chapter Three

1797

Liberty and Equality, both were possible, what he doubted was Fraternity. Philippe looked up from the pamphlet he was reading; was that step on the staircase Monsieur Guilléron? No, it was too heavy, it must be the maid with her pail. He looked down again at the page, the writer was wrong, in his experience people never helped each other unless there was a possibility that their aid would be returned. He had been taught to read because the tutor had said it would help his young master, actually it had been to keep the schoolmaster from losing his temper with that stupid boy. The boatman had fished him out of the water, hoping that it was somebody's lost cloak; Perrin had found him work to demonstrate his own benevolence. If necessary he would wear a cockade, he would risk a good deal for Equality, but Fraternity, that was a sugary word, flung in merely to delude the inexperienced.

He leaned his elbow on the table and a document crackled. It was supposed to be copied by noon on the following day but he could not bring himself to take up his pen. What could the measurements of a field and three outhouses mean to a mind that was ranging as far as the Orient? He only knew the places on the map, Smyrna, Alexandria, Aleppo, sometimes he changed the names but never the dream. He felt himself rocking, not in this little room in front of a cupboard full of deeds but out in a rowboat on a blue sea that in his imagination was as flat as the lake, turning a gold bezant over in his hands like the coin that an Italian merchant had once shown to Monsieur Guilléron, and calculating as he passed the anchored ships, what their cargoes would fetch and what he would do with his profits, buy a house at Lausanne, a vineyard at Morges, no, if once he got as far as the East, he would never return.

The first step was to reach a port but that required money. His exile was against him, he might be proscribed as an émigré if he crossed the frontier although he had been forced to come to Lausanne as a child and watch his mother die as a result. Yet the traders from Lyons and Nantes had left their little shops and their subservience inside them, to found their own empires in a dozen Mediterranean ports. Unlike some of the young Vaudois he knew, he had no wish to enter a regiment. His fortune waited him in the East, he knew it as clearly as if the crier had proclaimed it in the market place but how could he get to the city of his choice? Most of the people he met did not even know Aleppo existed.

Nobody had helped him but Mazelet. Who would imagine that an old shoemaker, hammering away in his dusty little shop, would have better information about France than they had in the gazettes. The man had only one idea in his head, the liberation of Vaud. "Why should they treat us as schoolchildren," the cobbler always grumbled, "they tell us when to lift our potatoes and what to think. Then our taxes go to a man who has never seen us simply because he happens to have been born in Berne."

Lausanne, Berne, neither city was his birthplace. Philippe Masson, he wrote his name down on a bit of paper lying on top of a ledger and started, realizing his wastefulness. Paper was too valuable to be used for any but a serious purpose;

if he wanted to scribble he had a slate. It was, he supposed, a sudden snatching at his own identity, an illusion that he could be a merchant with bills to settle and credits to collect. He looked round at the tiny room that was his prison for the greater part of the day and knew it was unlikely that he could ever be more than Guilléron's clerk. He had served his apprenticeship to disappointment yet philosopher though he believed himself to be, what was the life that apparently lay in front of him but an account book, a quill and perhaps a silver franc on New Year's Day to mark his strict devotion to duty?

The summers were bearable. There was light enough after work for him to take long walks among the hills and these sent him to sleep if they did nothing to ease his discontent. It was the winter he feared. He had the choice of warming himself beside the stove and listening to the tales of how his landlady's uncle had cheated her brother out of a load of firewood or shivering under an inadequate quilt at the top of the house while his illusions mocked him, "A clerk is always a clerk, how are you going to get even as far as Toulon."

It was time to return to his lodging unless he wished to miss his supper and he crumpled the bit of paper and put it in his pocket. Otherwise Guilléron would reprove him for his wastefulness in the morning.

How early it was getting dark! He would have to leave earlier or ask for a candle. As it was, he stumbled at the threshold over something hard, a pebble perhaps that had stuck to the sole of somebody's shoe and on an impulse he picked it up.

The object was not a stone. It was a heavy, gold earring. Treading on it seemed not to have scratched it, but who was the owner? It could not be Guilléron himself but they had had two visitors that day. One had been a farmer from near Ouchy who was anxious to buy another plot of land and the other a man Guilléron had distrusted, he claimed to be from Neuchâtel but they suspected he was French, who had offered them coffee at Rotterdam and also bales of cloth. He was probably the owner although he had said he was acting for another trader and mentioned that he was staying at the *Boeuf,* one of the smaller inns near the center of the town.

An earring! Philippe turned it over in his fingers; imagine giving away the profits of a season for such a toy! Only was it a toy? It could be an easy way to carry money in these disturbed days. Had the trader already discovered he had dropped it? He must take it back to him, he supposed, yet if he went now he would be late for his own supper and to wait might mean trouble with the watchman if he, a clerk, was out too long after dark. He hesitated and then, as he remembered afterwards, almost without making a conscious decision, he took the road up the hill towards the *Boeuf* instead of crossing it to go to his own lodging.

It was pleasant to be out in the air. The beginning of October had sometimes still a summer warmth. There were glimpses of gardens as he climbed, walnut trees with a nut or two still left on a branch, the last white roses sprawling over a wall. A boy ran past, followed by his dog, neighbors stopped to greet one another at the corner. The real cold would not begin for another month but the grass was bent as if preparing for the ice to come. At least the *Boeuf* was small, so the ostlers were less likely to be impertinent than their fellows at the bigger inns but to Philippe's relief as he came up to the door, the trader himself came out of it, evidently on his way to dine with friends in another part of the city.

"Excuse me, monsieur," Philippe tried to speak as deferentially as possible because nobody liked to admit a possible carelessness, "did you drop an earring when you came to visit us this afternoon?"

"An earring?" The man stared at him in such a bewildered way that Philippe wondered if he had used the right word.

"I found this on the staircase after you had left."

The merchant took the trinket in his hand and held it up to the light. After a moment, he scratched it with his nail as if he feared that it might be merely some substitute and then, very slowly, he opened his purse and took out its twin from a little linen bag. "How, I wonder, could I have dropped it?"

"I found it on the step outside my master's office."

"And why did you think it was mine?" The trader spoke so angrily that Philippe almost lost his temper. A thief would not have taken the trinket back to him.

"We had two visitors this afternoon. One was a farmer who would be unlikely to own a piece of jewelry and the other was yourself. I remembered you had told my master you were staying at the *Boeuf*."

"I am grateful to you. I bought the earrings for my wife," something in the tone made Philippe think this statement was a lie and then the trader added condescendingly, "you are honest."

"Otherwise I do not think Monsieur Guilléron would employ me."

The man put his hand into his purse but Philippe shook his head. "It is tradition here to give what service we can to the merchants who consult us." He liked the fellow less and less; now that he could listen to the accent in this silent street, he knew the man was French and an individual who would be a royalist in one town and a revolutionary in the next. He would certainly change his loyalties oftener than his cloak, a dusty garment that needed to be cleaned.

"At least let me offer you a glass of wine."

"But I think you are on your way to dine with friends."

"I am, but I am early and I should like to know what you, a Lausannois, think of the situation here," the trader's manner was now flattering and warm; "surely you will add to the kindness you have already shown me by sparing a few more minutes of your time."

Philippe bowed, his curiosity, the warmth that spread out of the door, tempted him to follow the trader to the nearest table and he noticed with gratification that a wine was ordered that was usually kept for a special occasion. "Business is stagnant at the moment," he felt that he was expected to comment on the situation in the city, "people who have a château in the country and a house in town are trying to sell one or the other to cover their expenses but at the moment there are few buyers."

"It will get worse till they forget their principles and are willing to deal with both sides in a conflict."

"Sometimes I wonder if they even know France is at war," Philippe was shocked at his indiscretion as the words burst out of him, "but they have their preoccupations."

"If they don't, they will know soon enough. The French are inside Cairo now and who can tell what riches they have found there? The world is changing while Lausanne stands still, if one may alter the proverb a little. I fear your master will face many disappointments. If he had been willing to buy that coffee at Rotterdam, as I proposed this morning, and keep it for a year, he would make a fortune."

"And worried himself sick meanwhile over a possible drop in prices and rats in the warehouse."

"I know, I know, when they speak of riches they think of farms and vineyards, the very things that can most easily be taxed. If the prices rise in Lausanne, they rise in Berne as well and then Their Excellencies increase the dues. You can hide an earring," the trader took one out of his purse again and looked at it, "you can't hide an ear of corn."

"Nothing seems to happen here from one generation to the next," Philippe took another sip of wine. It was one that he had tasted before only when a client had built a new house and invited them all to celebrate its completion.

"I would willingly stay another week. Not for the company, our friends, as you say, keep repeating the opinions of the grandfathers, but for the climate. It is pleasant to see the grass and a few last apples hanging in the sun after a summer of dusty journeys. But I must get down to Toulon before the bad weather begins, there are cargoes and opportunities there beyond any trader's dreams."

Philippe hardly heard the words but he knew that a chance was hovering in front of him. He looked at the wall, it was blank, there was nothing on it, not a picture nor a scribbled word, to influence him in one way or another. The street corner, his mother's death, the freezing water closing over his head, flashed and merged in a sequence of memories. He was sure of a room, bread in the morning and soup at night, if he got up, bowed and said farewell. The trader was looking at him, now obviously in a hurry, he distrusted the man but opportunities were seldom offered twice. Once he had addressed an envelope to a Swiss in Constantinople. He had wondered then as he was wondering now through what hands it would pass before it reached the merchant whose name he had written on the paper. He looked up in desperation at the wall. The decision depended only on himself. The trader was paying for the wine, the moment stretched but the silence could not go on, the man was about to rise from the table. "I suppose, monsieur, you would not require a clerk?" Philippe felt himself trembling as the words slipped out, his emotions were unsteady rather than his will and he grasped instinctively the edge of the table.

"A clerk?" The man looked at him sharply. "But what experience have you had apart from copying deeds about the sale of a row of vines measured by six peasants and disputed by the rest of the village."

"Oh, we have done much business with merchants in Holland and," Philippe paused a moment because it had been an isolated experience, "with the Swiss in Constantinople."

"Oh, that is more interesting. But I am merely a traveler, I go here and there wherever there is business to be had. You won't get rich with me; still you are an honest youth and I see you are ambitious." He could drop the fool directly he got to Toulon and he had been wondering if he should not engage a boy to guard the baggage during the difficult journey through France. "But what about your master? Are you bound to him?"

"I am a clerk. I was never an apprentice."

"But what will he say? I want no trouble here."

"Let me join you at the next village. I will leave a letter saying I am anxious to trace my relatives in France because I should not want him to think me lacking in gratitude (for what?—a cold room, a little food, much copying and no chance of advancement?) but Monsieur Guilléron can easily find someone to replace me. Only I have no papers."

"What are you? An émigré?"

"No, monsieur, I was born in France but my parents were honest citizens. After my father died, my mother was offered work here." It was, Philippe told himself, almost true.

"I was told when I bought these earrings that they were lucky; perhaps the finding of this," he held the little speck of gold up to the light again, "will bring you fortune. I can ask for papers for my servant," it would mean a bribe but a comparatively small one, "only remember that travel is as insidious as a woman although far more rewarding than Monsieur Guilléron's philosophical speculations."

"Where and when do you wish me to join you?"

The idiot! The trader looked Philippe up and down, the young fool could not keep the eagerness out of his face. Imagine giving up solid employment for fever, possible starvation and the dirty outskirts of some unsavory port! He had not even asked him about wages. Still he had proof that the fellow was honest and he could dismiss him promptly once he had no further use for him.

"I am going first to Lyons. Join me at the *Café des Raisins* at Écublens at noon on Wednesday. But remember, I want no trouble with the authorities or your master."

Five days. How much easier it would have been to snatch up his few possessions and follow his new employer the next morning. However, it would give him time to get a warm coat with his few savings and if there were enough, a pair of boots. "How can I thank you," he did not notice that the trader was looking at him almost with contempt, "I shall be with you on Wednesday and waiting for your orders."

Chapter Four

1797

It was a clear October day and usually Antoine would have had better things to do than to walk up at his father's bidding to invite his aunt and her daughter, Sophie, to dinner the next Sunday. It was a dreary occasion for them all but it was a rule that once a month they had to eat together. He suspected that it was so that they could be lectured about the sins of the young, sometimes they almost giggled when the same idiotic phrases were used time after time; "There is no diligence"—it would be said with such emphasis that the carving knife would slip and gravy would splash over the clean, white tablecloth; or even more often, "Careless children never realize the sacrifices that their parents make for them."

He kicked a pebble across the path. He ought to be enjoying himself now that those dreary hours at the College were over but instead of being willing to buy him a commission so that he could travel and enjoy new experiences, his father intended to bind him to a notary at Morges and then take him into his own business. All the man did was to buy land, grapes or cheese and it would be four years of copying figures. Besides, long before his apprenticeship was over, Vaud was going to change. He had already joined a club or circle as they called it here so that he and his fellow rebels would be ready to shake off the yoke of Berne and join the Revolution. For a moment he wondered why they spoke of a yoke? The word brought a picture of two patient oxen trundling along a furrow and "the Bears" were neither oxlike nor patient. Soon, so soon, Lausanne would be free but would that day come in time to save him from the notary's office?

He would have made an excuse to slip away but the walk fitted in with his own plans. Louis, the leader of their circle, had asked him the previous day to find out from Jean Michel, and he lived only ten minutes away from his aunt, if some leaflets had arrived from France. "We shall need one for the meeting on Saturday and Mazelet is waiting for them, they were due last week." The leaflets were among the most useful weapons they had, wonderfully designed so that on the surface they appeared to be religious exhortations.

"Remember," Louis had said almost fiercely the night before, "under no circumstances are you to deliver them yourself. If you were stopped, you could implicate the lot of us."

"Sophie!" Madame Perrin hurried toward the end of the garden, "Sophie! Don't hide yourself, Antoine is here. He has brought us a wonderful piece of cheese from your uncle and you can walk back with him as far as the end of the road if you like."

Did it mean an invitation for Sunday? How Sophie hated those dreary occasions in spite of the food. It involved sitting in her best clothes in complete silence when she might have been playing with Henriette at the neighboring farm. Besides, afterwards her mother always scolded her.

"Only if you would like to come with me." Antoine was carrying his hat under his arm and an empty basket was dangling from his wrist. It had become a custom that whenever he came with a message, Sophie would walk back a part of the way with him and he could send her home before they got to Jean Michel's vineyard. She nodded but then as

Madame Perrin held open the gate for them, Antoine bowed to his aunt and added as she had feared, "We shall expect you both directly church is over next week."

"Tell me some news," Sophie begged as soon as they were out of earshot of the house; her cousin was her only direct contact with the world, otherwise it was a matter of hearing scraps of sentences from the far end of her uncle's room while the women round her talked about embroidery.

"News! The news that concerns me is that my father wants me to go to some dreary counting house at Morges now that I have finished at the College. Can you imagine it! The days I might be out fishing I shall have to spend copying figures into a ledger."

"Oh, I should like to be a merchant and visit strange lands."

"That's impossible, Sophie, if you want to make voyages you will have to marry a sea captain."

"And why can't I be a trader?"

"You will understand why when you are older."

"Why not now? I am twelve."

Antoine could not have been more tiresome. He walked half a zigzag along the path without saying a word. "Men would pay you compliments," he muttered at last, "but they would not trust their goods to you. Trading is not as simple as sowing lettuces or picking grapes."

"Don't tell a *vigneron* vines are simple," and they both laughed.

"Let's talk about something else, I've got to see Jean Michel and once we get there, you must go back to your mother."

"The French said women were to have the same rights as men."

"But that was in 1791 and it didn't last. It's true that women are doing different tasks in France but that is due to the war and the men being in the army. They are simply doing the best they can for their husbands."

"We are serfs. You use us when necessary and otherwise treat us like dolls."

"Who has been putting such ideas into your head? What would my father say if he heard you?"

"Say?" Sophie shrugged her shoulders, they had to smash the present pattern of life. "Say? He would box my ears."

"Seriously, Sophie, who has been talking to you about the Revolution?"

"Nobody. I worked it out for myself. But the words are in the air." She glanced round, the vineyard they were passing was empty and she yelled into Antoine's ear, *"Vive Égalité, vive le Pays de Vaud."*

"You must tell me who it was. You will get your mother into trouble if they hear you."

"It's in the air, they mutter it at the fountains, it passes round with a basket of fruit."

"I did not know the movement was so widespread." Antoine stopped and looked behind him anxiously. Below him the port was full of boats. The water was neither blue nor green but the mixed colors, Sophie thought, of her mother's old London shawl.

"Do remember, Sophie, you are in a dangerous position. Your mother cannot afford to pay a heavy fine."

"Not with sugar at twenty batz the pound."

They laughed together as if they were joint conspirators. It was impossible, as Sophie knew from experience, to be angry with her cousin for long. "Are you going to talk with Jean Michel about Berne? His wife thinks as I do and she trusts me."

"It's more than time you went back to your weeding. There is Jean Michel coming to meet us." Perhaps some instinct warned Sophie not to turn but she dropped a pace or two behind her cousin when he greeted the *vigneron.*

"Matthieu is ill," Jean Michel began before he noticed her.

"Ill or . . . ?"

"Really ill. He got wet a few nights ago and it brought back that stiffness in his knee. He can't walk at present."

"That makes it difficult."

"Particularly as the tracts arrived last night."

Tracts? Sophie stared at her cousin. Jean Michel was noted for his irreligious views and Antoine had been sternly reproved by his father one Sunday for falling asleep during a Bible reading. Tracts? "Oh, they disguise those leaflets, you know, as texts," a remark Uncle Laurent had once made flashed through her mind. "Do you need a messenger? Let me take them."

"You!" Jean Michel who had not noticed Sophie till that moment, stared suspiciously at her face.

"Yes, why shouldn't she take them down?" Whatever the tracts were, Antoine seemed to know all about them. "She talks to your wife and I will vouch for her. Why, she's been shouting *'Égalité'* at me all down the hill."

"But she's a child."

"All the less likely, therefore, to be stopped. Sophie, can we trust you to take a basket from here to Lausanne without looking inside it or saying a word about your adventure afterwards?"

It was so unexpected that Sophie felt that her excitement would stifle her but she managed to stutter *"Salut, citoyen"* and shake Jean Michel by the hand. "You're the foreigner's child," he murmured, "but liberty knows no frontiers. How can you explain your absence to your mother?"

"She told me that I might join my friend Henriette to look for the last berries tomorrow morning."

"Very well," Jean Michel looked at her sternly, "come to my house instead but be careful. The best time is about an hour after the men have gone to the fields and before the women go a second time to the fountain."

Everything was hazardous but it was the way Sophie liked it to be. She might have overslept, she might not have persuaded her mother there were still a few berries to be found on the hedges, somebody might have told them at home that she had not turned beside the walnut tree to go to the farm and later Uncle Laurent might catch sight of her, walking through Lausanne. Jean Michel was already in the garden, leaning on the fence. "You are sure nobody saw you leave?" he asked suspiciously as he led her into a shed where Marie was stuffing the texts into an old basket. Sophie shook her head and looked down at a line, "the fruits of your toil go to those who have not earned them," but Marie put her hand over the paper. "Don't read it now," she advised, "you must be able to swear that you do not know what you are carrying if you are stopped. I can give you one to read once you are safely back." It had not occurred to Sophie that she could be questioned but Jean Michel said hastily, "There is no need to be afraid. Just walk naturally and nobody will notice you."

"I was only frightened of not getting here in time." They would not ask a boy if he were scared. Why should they ask her?

"And don't start looking either as if you had pinned a green cockade on your shawl."

Her cockade was already in her heart. She could not move nor think without flaunting it.

"Not too many, Marie, they are heavier than they look and she won't be able to carry them." Jean Michel spread a cloth above the leaflets and then filled the basket up with greens and a freshly baked loaf. "Do you know where Monsieur Mazelet lives?"

"The shoemaker in the alley opposite Suzanne's stall in the market?"

"You mean the apple woman, I suppose, but have you actually seen Mazelet?"

"I have not spoken to him but I have often passed his shop."

"Tell him to eat the bread but I should like to have the basket back at his convenience."

Sophie lifted her load, it weighed more than she had expected, and started toward the gate. "Wait a moment," Marie wiped her dusty hands on her apron, "our neighbor's eyes are always on this garden. It is sheer curiosity, I think, but let me find out if she is watching the gate now."

"Is it too heavy for you?" Jean Michel looked at her anxiously, "I would have carried it to the outskirts of Lausanne but we must not be seen together."

"No, I'm used to weights. We go to a farm most summers to help with the haymaking."

"Quick, Sophie, the old woman's feeding her chickens and she can't see you from the back yard."

"Give Mazelet this," Jean Michel pushed a scrap of torn ribbon into her hand, "and tell him I had good news from Nyon."

Sophie waved and started down the hill at a good pace, knowing that she would not exchange the moment for a whole summer in the mountains. She was not afraid of the police, only a little of her mother. It would take her almost an hour to reach the cobbler and rather longer to get back because it would be uphill. If her mother went to look for her and found her off on an errand of her own, she would never be allowed to leave the house again alone and all hope of helping the Revolution would be over.

It was still warm. Both ends of a scarlet headcloth flapped against a woman's back as she weeded her garden. Some girls waved to her, they were hanging up sheets and a small, white nightcap, it looked forlorn among the billowing linen, to dry on a line and far below her, old François was leading his donkey, a small barrel strapped to each side of the animal, to fetch water from the lake for his plants.

The gardens gradually grew smaller, a sign that she was nearly at the city and by now she saw the cathedral on the opposite hill. A low wall in front of a house tempted her to rest her basket on it for a moment and as she did so she noticed that two or three apples scattered about a tree were almost the same red as the tiles on the roof. It reminded her of her mother's care in matching patterns, she herself did not mind whether things were the same colors or not. It was good to be alone and free to act as it pleased her but then she heard footsteps and caught sight of a man's silver shoe buckles as he came down some steps. She jumped up, she was outside the garden but she must not start dreaming until her errand was completed. The roads grew more and more crowded the nearer she came to the market. Wheels clanged on the cobbles, harness rattled, dogs growled, it was, as Antoine always said, a series of thunderclaps broken by yells. In a few moments she had to dodge between the lines of red or blue and white aprons put out to tempt the women who would soon have to thin the grapes and the piles of *tommes,* the pale mountain cheeses that were said to be strengthening in the spring after a dark winter. To reach Monsieur Mazelet's alley she had to pass by Suzanne's stall. Suzanne was a friend and famous for her Bussigny apples, her mother bought a tub of them every year and as she came closer to the stand she noticed that all the baskets except one were empty.

"Salut!" It was safer to speak than to risk Suzanne noticing her and complaining to her mother about her daughter's rudeness.

"Salut! Why, I haven't seen you since April. How have you passed the summer?"

"It was colder than usual. And there was not much fruit."

"Very little, but tell your mother her apples are waiting for her whenever she wishes to fetch them." The dome on the straw hat that was always perched a little sideways on Suzanne's head was like a child's top. As a small child, Sophie had always longed to cut it off and spin it.

"Apples . . . fine apples . . ." Suzanne turned to a passer-by in a long gray coat with a cane in his hand. He took the fruit she held out to him, lifted it haughtily, turned it round and put it back in her hand.

"Who does he think he is!" Suzanne looked angrily at the rejected apple and then at the figure walking toward the next stall. "A Bernois! An aristocrat! But did you smell the grease under all that powder on his hair?"

Sophie grinned. The man was a portrait of the landowners that her leaflets attacked.

"Apples, the best Bussigny apples. . . ."

"Not all the Bussigny apples are as good as you pretend," this time the man was an honest saddler and the bargaining would be serious. "Goodbye," Sophie said hastily, it was a splendid opportunity to slip away before she was given any more messages or questioned about the health of various relatives. Suzanne was so absorbed by her prospective sale that she merely nodded. Sophie walked past the stalls, across to the last line of peasants, poorer people who stood or sat on little stools behind a bundle of wooden pegs for the garden or the tiny bags of dried mountain plants reputed to cure coughs instantly if mixed with a glass of old wine although according to Uncle Laurent, if the drinks were of value it was the wine rather than what he described as the grasses, on and on until she came finally to the cake stall at the corner. The smell of the spices was so comforting, her regret that she did not even have a batz with her to buy a simple cake so absorbing, that she bumped into two watchmen standing at the bottom of Mazelet's street.

"Where are you going, girl," one of them said angrily, "and what have you got in that basket of yours? It's too heavy to be full of greens."

"Just a loaf of bread. I'm taking it to my grandmother."

One of the men put out his hand and Sophie expected him to turn the basket over on the stones. He would not consider the leaflets to be tracts. Her clothes were sticking to her back, a woman coming down the hill with a bunch of wildflowers in her hand looked at her curiously and almost stopped, the market suddenly seemed full of noise. "Please, please . . . ," she noticed with astonishing clarity the dozen veins in a cabbage leaf squashed between two cobbles. Perhaps her genuine bewilderment saved her? She had purposely put on her most faded dress and looked what she was supposed to be, a girl from a distant village. "Off with you but next time look where you are going," the taller of the two men laughed, "and be out of here before the market ends, then the square will be full of horses and they'll startle you."

Now she dared not go straight up the alley but would have to climb the second, broader street and approach Mazelet's shop from the upper end. It was a moment to swing the basket to show how light it really was but it hung like a weight on her arm. The men might be watching her, could they see the papers through the wicker, the handle rubbed her arm, she expected a shout. Suddenly she thought of her mother, what would happen if she were summoned to a guard-room to answer questions about her daughter's activities? Nobody would believe that her mother was innocent. Must every action involve others in its course? Antoine, Jean Michel and Marie, would a moment's carelessness destroy them all? It seemed a league to the corner although it could not have been a hundred steps. It was risky to turn her head but she could not resist glancing back when she came to the end of the street. The two men were still standing in the same place but they had their backs to her.

In sheer relief, the word freedom rang through her head as she started to climb the hill. Her mother had left home to follow her father but now that she was alone and unable to earn a few *louis* like a man, she might never see her family and her own country again. Berne was like Uncle Laurent. Its subjects, like bushes, were to grow and die in the same spot but not all people were alike. Antoine wanted to go overseas, she wanted to learn. They could say what they liked about the Revolution in France, it had given the people more liberty. There were too many laws here, too much order, and far too much talk about Reason.

Mazelet's shop seemed farther and farther away as Sophie tramped down a narrow alley that was slippery with vegetable leaves and refuse. It must have been months since anybody had cleaned the street. The air was heavy and she was thankful, as she had been so often, that they did not live in Lausanne. She stopped, had she passed the door? No, there was his sign at last, not twenty paces away (could she have taken the direct road) from the place where the watchmen had stopped her.

Mazelet was studying a pair of old riding boots that stood in front of him on a long and much scarred table. He looked up with the irritated expression Uncle Laurent had if disturbed in his pruning. Sophie stood still a moment and he glanced at the row of mended shoes along a shelf on the wall. Then she put the torn, green bit of ribbon into his hand and said proudly, *"Égalité, citoyen."*

"So even children are in the game." He took the other half of the ribbon from the bottom of an earthenware pot and fitted the two scraps together. "Well, what news have you brought me?"

"Jean Michel has had good news from Nyon and my basket is full of leaflets. The bread and greens are for you but he would like the basket back at your convenience."

"He shall have it on Sunday. And now, you have had a long walk, let me give you a slice of the bread."

"Thank you, no," Sophie was hungry but she knew it was merely politeness, he would not want to cut the loaf before supper. "I must get back as soon as possible. Some of our neighbors favor Berne."

"All things take time, even mending shoes. Remember, but Jean Michel will have told you, if we happen to meet again, we have never seen each other before." He held the door open, looked out and motioned her to go. It was disappointing that he had not said a single word about the Revolution but the smell of leather and the sounds of the market square would be symbols of adventure to her as long as she lived. *"Au revoir."* She wished he had said *"Égalité"* but almost before she had stepped across the threshold, he was back at his table and bent over his work.

Chapter Five

"My master would have liked to fit the coat again." The apprentice looked about thirteen although he was actually older and in the striped linen jacket and breeches in which his master dressed him, he needed only a hat tucked under his arm to appear some gentleman's son waiting for his tutor. He was staring neither at Antoine nor the garment that he had brought with him but at a cupboard at the end of the room, less because he was interested in its contents than to show his indifference toward a tiresome young man who was a customer only because his father could afford to pay some extremely expensive bills.

"I have been invited unexpectedly to a family celebration so please take my old coat round to our house this evening." Antoine put his hand into his pocket, found a small coin and thrust it into the urchin's hand. He had already dressed himself in what was to have been his clean Sunday shirt and his best breeches because he intended to wear the new coat as an omen of the future at the meeting he was to attend that afternoon. His father would not approve of the color when he saw it; black, they had agreed, would be too somber but his father had advised a dark gray whereas Antoine had picked the blue that was now so fashionable in France and not, as they would say in the family, serious. Yet he was a man and they were still treating him as a boy. Only his membership in the secret club that Louis had founded kept him alive among such irritating frustrations.

The meetings were held in a deserted hut on a hill above the city and the one to which he was now bound should be particularly interesting because Louis was going to read a report newly smuggled in from France. It was growing late. He would have to hurry. He snatched up the coat, he could never be sure afterward what precisely happened, but a large button caught in the rush-backed chair, the thread snapped and it lay, a tiny, round wheel, directly on the floor in front of him. "It was never sewn on properly," he stormed, stamping his feet in annoyance. Now he would miss the opening speech because it would take a journeyman five minutes at least to sew it on for him.

The apprentice disappeared with the garment and Antoine sat down indignantly in the chair. It was seldom that he had a holiday on Saturday, his father found so many errands for him, and here he was, wasting time in a stupid shop. Oh, how things irritated him in Lausanne, customs were rigid, people were old. Life had renewed itself the other side of the frontier and that was why the Lausannois were afraid to speak about France. There had been excesses at the beginning, he agreed, what could people expect after generations of tyranny, but there was a life in the pamphlets, even when it was hidden under dull religious advice, that was lacking in the citizens here. Was it because a youth there could be what he wished and not the copy of his father? He ran his fingers along his waistcoat as if fingering an imaginary cockade.

Take his coat, for example (how slow that boy was, what were they doing about that button?), it was really a new color. "A gentleman does not go about looking like a popinjay," his father had said the previous Sunday about a young man who had merely worn a flowered waistcoat in the French fashion instead of the plain colors and black breeches of his elders. Who wanted to repeat the same style all his life? If they were supposed to have a uniform then let it be a gay one like those the French officers wore when they were recruiting peasants for their army. Oh, it was not clothes alone but ideas, not his father only but "the Bears." Every avenue was blocked to him, success, riches, adventure simply because of the place of his birth.

"Let me help you on with it." The apprentice was back with a flat expression on his face that just concealed his native insolence, holding the mended garment in his outstretched hands. He was wondering if he would get another batz but by now Antoine was too frustrated to think of it.

"You are sure you cannot wait for my master to see it?" Imagine the fool buying something so expensive and then rushing off without a final fitting!

"I have told you, I am summoned to a celebration."

The handle of the door slipped from Antoine's fingers and it slammed behind him. Usually he would have apologized for the apparent rudeness but today the bang expressed his feelings. Did his father really think that he would go to that counting house at Morges, a day's ride from all his friends and he would not have the money for a horse, to spend four years copying figures? Louis had promised to see if there were a way to help him and if he failed, there was always the recruiting officer, although he did not like the prospect of marching up and down a yard while he was yelled at by a sergeant. He glanced proudly down at his coat and then, pride today seemed to be matched with annoyance, he remembered that he still had the crowns in his purse that his father had given him to pay the tailor and that now he would have to go all the way back by the shop to do this after the meeting was over.

He was hot by the time he had walked briskly up the hill

and he thought guiltily for a moment how pleasant it would be to race down to the shore so far below him and sit there till the sun set over Geneva in all the scarlet splendor of an officer's sash. His favorite bay, outlined by poplars, was so much in his mind that he almost collided with a citizen, hurrying in the opposite direction. "Look where you are going," the man said pleasantly, "but turn if you are out for a walk. There's some disturbance up there and the watch has arrived. Can't you hear the shouts?"

Antoine hesitated, he could hear some yells but it was probably a pair of drunken peasants who had started a fight. If he swept round to reach the hut from the farther side, Louis would probably have finished the report before he arrived. He decided to go on but before he turned the corner a youth came racing toward him. "Run," he gasped, "they've arrested the others." It was Henri, the son of a lawyer who knew his father and who had been a member of the club from the beginning.

"Arrested them!"

"Run!" Henri grabbed him by the sleeve, there were cries behind them and they could hear the thud of heavy boots on the path. Arrested! Why? Was it a crime to talk about France? He dodged under a branch. Must clutch his hat. A fallen hat could betray him. Dungeons. Tales by the fire. A white face staring up at him from stinking straw. (And that's what happens to disobedient boys!) There was no air. Henri was running faster than he was, oh, that root! He might have stumbled over it if he had not seen it just in time. He must stop, he could not breathe, Henri was jumping over bushes, scrambling down a bank, "Here," he panted and there, in a hollow with trees all round it, at least for the moment they were safe.

"I was on guard one side and Paul the other," Henri gasped as they recovered their breath. "It was a nightmare. I suddenly saw a man strike Paul in the face so I yelled a warning and ran. I doubt if many got away from the hut."

"Somebody must have betrayed us."

"We met too often in the same place to say the same things."

"Did Louis have a list of our names?"

"No, he always said it wasn't safe. He was at the back near the window, he may have got away but whoever betrayed us to the watch probably knew who we were."

An ant was crawling over a stone, tiny white stars of lichen looked as if they were paint, a triumphant afternoon dissolved precipitately into menace and terror. Somewhere an animal rustled through the undergrowth and they both jumped. Their companions were being led roughly to the guardhouse and at any moment some pursuer might seize them by the collar. "Let's get away before they search this wood," Henri dusted his hat with his sleeve, "there's a garden near here where we can hide."

They passed the stump of a tree, the bushes ended abruptly and they ran down an easy slope till they came to a low wall round what appeared to be a deserted house. To Antoine's surprise Henri leaned over the gate and pulled back the bolt. "You need not be afraid, my father knows the owner and he is spending a month in the country with his brother. He left the old cook in charge but she is sure to be asleep this hot afternoon. They are unlikely to look for us here." He led the way cautiously across a kitchen garden, jumped over a bed of carrots, opened another gate and flung himself under the first apple tree growing in the orchard. A muffled noise startled them but it was only the wheels of an old wagon grinding along the neighboring road. Two dark roses, the dusk brought out their fragrance as if to mock them, hung over a wall. They lay in this backwater of grass and shade as if submerged in the lake until Antoine finally roused himself.

"What are we going to do?" he asked although Henri was a year younger than himself.

Henri did not reply. He seemed to be interested in a dandelion and kept running his fingers up and down its stem. "It depends upon the watch," he said finally, "Louis will not talk but some of the others may. The best thing is to go to our families at once. We can tell them that when we joined the club we did not know it had any political aims. We left it as soon as this was apparent and we were not there this afternoon."

"But how can we prove our absence?"

"Leave that to my father. He will be angry but unlike Monsieur Perrin he does not love Berne. He has to be careful in his position what he says but I know his real feelings."

"No!" Antoine smacked the ground with his fist, unfortunately hitting a thistle but even its pricks seemed a symbol of liberty. The counting house at Morges, the restrictions at home, tumbled away like a torn-up paper in the wind now that the watch was searching for him. He had prayed for freedom. It was being offered to him. "No, I have had enough of tyranny. I shall leave for France," he sprang to his feet, "at once."

"But have you got any money?" Henri, like his father was so practical.

"No," he never had more than a batz or two in his pocket but then he remembered, "oh, yes, I have. I was to have paid the tailor for this coat and forgot."

"It was lucky you were late."

"Late?" Then he remembered the button; that loose thread that he had cursed so heartily had saved him. "Yes, I suppose I was."

"Be sensible, Antoine, let the matter die down. Louis kept no list, he was probably at the table and if so near the window.

He may have got away. They will only have the words of some frightened youths for evidence and if we go to my father at once, he will swear, I am sure, that we spent the afternoon with him."

"And lie!" Yet it was not a falsehood that was the impediment, the thought that filled his head was freedom. It was a rainbow, a summer night, threads of blue lake between the rustling leaves, all that he loved and thought of as liberty. Unless he took his chance and took it now, he would stick in that counting house for the rest of his days.

"But Antoine, think of your opportunities," Henri had been jealous of his friend's future for months. A solid training, the chance to become a merchant, think to what it could lead! He saw himself saving every crown that came his way and eventually, but not, he thought, till he was thirty, finding a girl to marry, some elder daughter with a good dowry and then taking his place among the chief citizens of the town. As it was at present, it was uncertain if his father could even afford the fees for him to study law.

"I do not intend to bury myself at Morges."

"But you can't set off to France as you are. You have no passport."

It was true, Antoine looked down at the sleeve of his by now dusty coat, the blue was too light, the cut too elegant for such a journey. Then, as if everything was combining to strengthen his resolve, he remembered Jean Michel. "I have a friend who will help me but I must get to him before they search the roads. Perhaps, later on, you could tell my father what happened."

"We must get you away." Jean Michel's fingers traced the knots on the wood of the table in front of them as if they were a map, "but how and where?"

"I can walk into France."

"Without papers?"

Oh, why should life revolve eternally around passports! The worthy citizen . . . the honest citizen . . . soon a person would need a permit to visit his own farm! Yet it only required will and a man could get what he wanted as the rebels in France had shown. How would he cross the frontier? Why, he could crawl across the fields at night. What would he do when he got there? Find a young man his own age who would sympathize with his aspirations. They would shout *"Vive la Liberté"* together and the next morning his new friend would whisper a word into some trader's ear and then ride, or if necessary walk, with him to Paris. "There are ways, I know," and he looked triumphantly at Jean Michel.

"You would be arrested before you had gone a day's march from here." It was not that he was unsympathetic; they needed these youths with their enthusiasms if they wanted to remake the canton but the *vigneron* was also tired of eager boys who were rebels because of their age and not because they understood the meaning behind the word, revolution. "Have you no friends outside Lausanne who would shelter you for a time?"

"No." Antoine's dream of France was too strong to allow him even to contemplate another solution.

"Think again. Otherwise I shall have to send you back to your father. The last peddler I could trust left a week ago. If only I knew someone in Neuchâtel. It's easier to get there." Jean Michel scratched his head. It would be to his advantage to get the boy away because he was obviously too inexperienced to hold out long against the efficient questioning of either his father or the magistrates and then he feared the disclosure of his own careful and patient work.

"Neuchâtel! But I do know somebody there. A Monsieur

Roulet. He is a distant cousin of my father and he spent a month with us two summers ago. He never talked about politics if people were there but sometimes when we were alone, he joked about 'the Bears' and then put his finger to his lips."

"Would he take you in?"

"Oh, yes, but I want to go to Paris."

"Spend the winter with your kinsman and if he is sympathetic, he may be able to get you proper papers for your journey next April. I can find you a guide to take you to Estavayer, it is on the lake almost opposite Neuchâtel. Now let us count your money. You will need different clothes," he looked scornfully at Antoine's coat, "a guard could see that blue a meadow away and it's unwise to look like a prosperous citizen. The fishermen who will row you across will ask a *louis* if not more, they seized a man last May and confiscated his boat because he had a fugitive on board, and there will be food for the journey. I know you are disappointed," Antoine was staring at him bleakly, "but one thing neither of us can do is to change the season. I might have been able to get you to France in May but not when it is already October."

"One *louis,*" the man said quietly, his elbows on the table.

"But where should I find such a sum?" Antoine leaned across his small bundle. By now his breeches and shoes were white with dust.

"It's dangerous work, taking you fugitives across the lake. What happens to them if they catch me?" He pointed to several children, all of them filthy and quarreling with one another, just outside the open door.

"I'll give you all I have," Antoine put two crowns upon the table.

"You believe in equality, don't you," the man sneered, "how much have you got in your hatband?"

"Not even a batz." He hated to put the battered felt on the dirty table but he pushed it over to the peasant so that the man could run his fingers round the brim. "Besides, I'm not a political, I got into trouble over a girl."

"A girl!" The man stared at him and laughed. "For this once I'll believe you. So you want to disappear."

"It will be safer for me to be out of the way for a few months."

"Come, be frank, you want to catch up with the recruiting officer and make your fortune."

"No soldiers do that."

"It would be a pity for a gentleman as young as yourself to gasp out his life on a battlefield."

"It was a girl." He must remember, Jean Michel had warned him, never to show anxiety or impatience. Yet he wondered if he could stay in this stinking hut much longer? There was one bed where, it seemed, the whole family slept, this greasy table and three or four stools. He was a new victim and he could feel the fleas crawling around his neck and biting him and now there was even one up his sleeve, nipping him from elbow to shoulder. It was not the clean dirt of some cowshed in the mountains nor the hole that an animal might make in a tree but something inexpressibly degrading and evil. "It was a girl," he repeated with all the mournfulness he felt, "during the haymaking."

"Was she pretty?"

"Naturally, but then she said I had promised her marriage and I had never spoken of it," Antoine invented on the spur of the moment, "still if you cannot take me," he put his hands over the crowns, "I will walk on to the next village before it is dark." He got up, flung his bundle on his shoulder and took up his stick.

"Three *écus* and I will take you over tonight."

"Willingly if I had them but look," Antoine emptied his purse out on the table, there were a few loose coins besides the two crowns and to add to the truth of his story, a wisp of hair. (How had it got there, he wondered?) The fellow pushed the empty purse back to him and scooped the money up into the palm of his hand. "It would be a pity for you to fall into the hands of some miserly old mother but it's a favor, mind you, and if you get across I shall expect you to send me the other crown. I will take you to my brother as soon as it gets dark."

It seemed a long time till the sun went down although Antoine left the hut to escape the fleas and sat outside on a log. This was not the gay adventure that he had expected. It was the season that was to blame, in June he could have tramped easily as far as Dijon, he knew people would have helped him. Now the same dreary thoughts went round and round in his head, had they caught Louis, who had told his father? The first law that he would make if he were a magistrate would be that a son was free to choose his own profession. If it had not been for the threat of that counting house this precipitate flight need not have happened.

What had become of his new coat? Jean Michel had hidden it away but when now would he wear it? Had Henri convinced his own father that they had not known the club to be political? After all, they had both of them spoken in the debates. There were so many questions and now he might never know the answers to them; besides, he had hidden the rest of his money in his shoe and how was he going to take it out without the peasant seeing him? Before he could solve the problem the guide came and tapped him on the shoulder.

"Move as quietly as you can and try not to break any twigs."

If it had not been for the circumstances Antoine would have enjoyed the walk. They scrambled through bushes but he managed to hide behind one of them long enough to rescue the last crown he had from its hiding place. They kicked old pine cones out of the way, passed a tree cut the previous year, the white edges were fading gradually into green as the ivy crept up the stump, and paused once while the guide listened to a sudden noise. The air was scented with late grass, so different from the decaying vegetable smells after the market had ended at Lausanne. It made him drowsy, he longed for a clean bed and food that was not full of flies. He tried to remember Monsieur Roulet; the man had been kind to him and had often given him a cake.

"Wait," his guide whispered, "now I must go and find my brother."

The ground was hard, suppose the man had taken his money and was going to leave him here? Neither the pamphlets nor the *Encyclopedia* had advice for a homeless fugitive lying on a stony bit of earth with the chill of an autumn night sinking into his bones. The lies he had had to tell! He was coming to believe in that farmer's daughter himself! What had happened to his friends? Had Henri's father been able to protect him? Were the others locked up in a cell? Above all, who had betrayed their club to the authorities? He heard a noise, he crawled forward, the grass seemed flatter when he had his face on it than it looked when he was standing up, and then the guide touched his shoulder. "My brother has agreed to take you but hurry. Don't stumble over a root or make a noise but come, the boat is ready."

It should have been a romantic parting from his native country but by the time Antoine was hauled aboard he was wet to the knees and that the water was a deep blackberry color under the pale moonlight was no consolation when one was shivering and hungry. It seemed an age before they reached the opposite shore and then they whispered he had five more miles to walk before he reached his kinsman's farm.

"And what, if I may ask this, are your plans?"

Antoine felt his kinsman's eyes moving downward from his mud stained collar to his broken shoes and he was uncertain if the man were laughing at him or angry. He had got here at the cost of cold, discomfort and more than apprehension, real terror, and it was for Roulet to make a suggestion. At the club, they had talked about the glories of Freedom and Opportunity; never about shivering in a bed of damp reeds with the real possibility that some nervous herdsman would set a savage dog on them.

"I don't know!" Why did his voice rise as if he were some small boy caught with fallen apples in his pocket and why must he notice so guiltily that his shoes had made muddy patches over the just-washed tiles?

"You should not play with politics unless you understand them."

But he did understand them. He knew more than this rigid farmer in front of him why he wanted to be free. It was because he was denied a career in the place where he happened to have been born. Perhaps, as some said, liberty made people lazy, and for all its adherence to Prussia, Neuchâtel had its own government. Such indifferent neighbors were another of the reasons why the Vaudois were treated like bondsmen. They sympathized, but they would not lift their hands, not here, not in free Neuchâtel, to help their brothers.

"We must be calm," Monsieur Roulet continued with exasperating slowness, "there are other dangers in the world besides Berne. I know what you are going to say, you might as well have become a *vigneron* instead of going to the College but conditions will change. Only it will take years yet and patience."

"We cannot and will not wait." If only he were back with his friends at the club, all longing for action, any action, that would get them away from their ledgers or grammars and the passivity of their elders.

"Yet look what has happened to you! A goatherd coming to his village after a summer in the mountains would be more presentable than you are at this moment. Still, since you have flung yourself on my mercy . . ."

"You are my kinsman."

"Only a very distant one but your father and I were friends as boys." (And a long time ago that must have been, Antoine ripped a thread out viciously from his torn pocket, and you won't make me believe that you sat with your Latin grammars or a sermon in front of you all Sundays.) "So I will keep you for the winter."

"I wish to cross into France."

"Reflect!" Monsieur Roulet's expression hovered between a grin and a taunt. "In a week or two the roads will be blocked and no recruiting sergeant enlists a man in October to eat his head off in a barrack room doing nothing. There may just be time to send a message to your father but you will have to stay here. By your own confession, you haven't a florin on you."

"I had to run for my life." Didn't the fool realize that it cost money to cross his wretched lake? "You do not understand what the Bernois did to us."

"I will ask Melanie to look out some old clothes and Jules to find you work. You can help him with the garden and the cows. It will be as rewarding in its way as cleaning your boots and keeping your temper if a sergeant bawls at you."

"I do not choose to be a peasant." He would walk if need be all the way to Paris and show the fool in front of him that he could give up everything for freedom.

"You will stay here." There was such a deliberate coldness in his kinsman's voice that he could never feel gratitude, no, not even if they gave him that so much hoped for hot meal. Monsieur Roulet walked across to the window and adjusted what appeared to be a perfectly straight curtain. "I shall not give you up to the authorities and if you work well, I will see what such friends as I have can suggest for you in the spring. Now come, I will take you to Melanie, I hope she can clean you up before we eat. Then perhaps," he looked down at the mud on the floor, "my daughters, your ever so distant cousins, may listen more sympathetically than I have to your ridiculous escapade."

It was again a cold winter. People said that the troubles in France had upset even the weather but looking up at the yellow tips of the firs, Antoine had to admit that he was not unhappy. Of course he resented being called out of a warm bed at six o'clock in the morning to help clean the stables but if he were working harder than he ever had in his life, at least it was with tools and not with ledgers. The snow fell, they cleared it away from the yard, the sun came out for a day and then there was another blizzard and the tub of water froze even outside the kitchen. Spring was as forbidden a word as revolution but then it was always winter and never spring for youth. He tried not to think about his father but he missed his companions and the surreptitious notes they had passed to each other in class, headed "For Liberty and Vaud." The Sundays were more austere than at Lausanne, there were no youths of his own age near the farm and Monsieur Roulet had apparently forbidden his daughters to talk to him except at meals. He picked up the broom he had dropped while he rubbed his fingers in their coarse mittens and then it was push, sweep, rake until the path was clear. It would not be for long. He looked up at the sky, it was a gray that he felt romantically was as bitter as his feelings about Roulet and knew that they would have another snow-storm by evening and that he was doing the work for nothing.

There was no desire for change at Neuchâtel. They wanted to live as they had in the time of their great-grandfathers. Roulet had bought the stableman a new kind of broom. The man had left it in a corner and gone on using an old stump until his master had got him another in the traditional pattern. Many people still believed potatoes to be a poison and destroyed the plants at night. Roulet had even said that unless he sowed the field himself, his men would throw away some new seed he had got from Amsterdam because it was strange to them. "Antoine can sow it," a neighbor had suggested and he had then overheard the troubling reply, "he may not be here at the right season." If only Monsieur Roulet could get him a commission or lend him the money to buy a horse! Yet the short days passed quickly doing his tasks and listening to tales in the evening, besides, like the squirrels in their tree trunks, he slept a lot. All he still resented was getting up at dawn; it felt as if he had swallowed an icicle when he crossed the frozen yard. Otherwise time was a snowy bridge that would melt in the spring when he would have to jump from it to one side or the other. Yet that was far off in the future, what mattered now was Melanie's hot soup and the thick quilt that he pulled over his ears at night. He swung his arms to get some warmth into them and picked up the broom, push, rake, sweep, hard work all of it, but better than to sit copying figures at a desk.

One day there was ice in the fountain and they broke it up

so that the birds could drink. The next day the air was lighter and somehow soft. The grass looked dead, there were patches of brittle leaves but people could hope. They turned the goats out to graze, then there was no difficulty in following the steep path that led to the next farm and a cluster of yellow flowers opened between two stones. The water in the stream still froze their hands if they dipped them into it but there was a general stirring everywhere until the day came when Monsieur Roulet saddled his horse and rode off to the first market; then they knew it was March.

They took up their favorite or allotted places round the stove waiting for Monsieur Roulet to finish his supper. He had returned late, bringing them all some small cakes from the town but it seemed rude to start eating them before he joined them. The girls argued for a moment about the best way to make a pancake and then stopped and even the herdsman forgot to repeat his dreary observations about the weather. On a hot summer day, he would still find something wrong with it. Antoine was restless, his kinsman would have gone to the notary to see if there were letters for him, it was safer having them sent there than to an outlying farm but the roads were still bad and it was unlikely that any news had come from his father in Lausanne. In a month's time, perhaps, he ought to cross into France before they had time to send him home.

"How silent you are! Don't you like the cakes?" Roulet came over finally from the table and sat down in his armchair opposite the stove.

"We were waiting for you to join us and tell us the news," Marie, his youngest daughter, looked up from her knitting.

"What news do you expect after a winter when all the armies were in their barracks? It's too early for the peddlers and their rumors. No, everyone had the same tale, it was a hard season, there had been disease among the cows and we are a week later than last year sowing the fields. But I saw Monsieur Gavillod, the notary, Antoine, and he gave me a letter from your father. A wagoner brought it to him just two days ago."

"Is he well?" It was a first instinctive question.

"Yes, although he writes it was a cold, difficult winter. He sends you his greetings but not yet his forgiveness, that, he says, will depend upon your future conduct."

"Did the authorities trouble him . . . about me?"

"Your membership of that ridiculous circle appears to have passed unperceived but several of your companions or rather their innocent parents, have been heavily fined."

"Did he tell you their names?"

"He did not use valuable space for so unimportant a detail."

"It's not unimportant to me!" Roulet was the most irritating person Antoine had met in his whole life. "I want to know what happened to my friends."

"You will have to be content with hearing that they were not dragged to Berne in irons. Their leader, it appears, jumped through a window and escaped." It was like Louis to have saved himself, he was agile and very thin.

"And what does my father propose?" He would not return to Lausanne, they would watch him every moment, forbid him to see his former schoolfellows and hurry him off, no doubt, to that office at Morges. If Roulet tried to send him back, he would slip away during the journey, he was wiser now than during his first, unpremeditated flight.

"You need not clench your fists, Antoine, your father agrees with me that it would be unwise for you to return home. I made a suggestion when I wrote him in the autumn and he has agreed to it. I have often told you about my friend, Mr. Robinson, who spent a year with me at the College at Yverdon."

"The Englishman who helped you to borrow a pony." To lure it from its pasture would have been a better description.

"I regret that at that time I was as unprincipled as you are now. He always asked me to send any son I had to him in London for a couple of years but as you see," and he glanced at them affectionately, "I have only daughters. I wrote to Robinson immediately after your arrival, we have always corresponded with each other, asking him if he could find you a respectable place in some merchant's office where you would not be entirely occupied with ledgers. It's a free country according to your ideas."

"But it never stops raining there."

"Now, Antoine, a good merchant never exaggerates. Besides, if you were one of Masséna's troopers you would sleep in a swamp and march over mountains."

"I prefer to go to France."

"Oh, Antoine, don't be foolish," Madame Roulet was so painfully matter-of-fact, "why do you want to get killed when it couldn't matter to you whether the battle was won or lost? France is not your native land."

"Robinson was the best horseman I have ever met and according to him, of course it is twenty years ago, London was full of attractive girls."

"Don't marry there, Antoine, remember you're a Vaudois."

"I have not accepted the offer." Yet he knew he would; think of the adventures he might meet on the journey, they would treat him as a man and not a boy and, this was not an inconsiderable factor in his decision, such merchants were rich and might give him the chance of earning some of those gold pieces that made the difference between helping with the cows or strolling in an embroidered coat, and always in the color of the year, down the main streets of a great city.

"You can rejoin your father after a few years if you feel that slavery at home is preferable to freedom abroad. By then your youthful escapades will have been forgotten. Be thrifty, Robinson's firm deals with the East, I believe, and he may put a bargain or two in your way. Save your guineas and you will be able to buy a house of your own when you return.

"He will end up a magistrate."

"No," Roulet smiled, "whatever London teaches him—and there, they say, the merchants wear silk stockings to their offices—I doubt if he will swear allegiance to Berne. Besides, there are changes in the air. Liberty, Antoine, may be slow but it could come to Vaud sooner than you think."

"Change?" He looked at the herdsman nodding drowsily by the stove and at Marie who was staring at him with respect. Nothing, it seemed, would ever be as simple as life had been only ten minutes ago. "I shall not have to spend my days with ledgers?" he checked.

"I made it clear you had a special aversion to them."

"When do I start?" It would probably be months before he had to make his preparations and there would be plenty of time to turn the offer over in his mind while he watched the roses open and the cattle leave for the mountains.

"As soon as we can get you some clothes and find the right traveling companions. I warned Robinson when I wrote to expect you early in the summer. If he has no vacancy himself, he has influence enough to place you with one of his friends. I am not going to wait for a reply from him, between fighting and the privateers half the letters get lost."

Chapter Six

Sophie woke suddenly, shivering from the cold. What were those heaps lying between her and the wall? Then she remembered, they were two of her schoolfellows, naturally the ones she liked the least. Madame Berthoud had confiscated the padded quilt that her mother had given her because she had spoken by chance in the corridor on the previous day. It was still dark, she could not swing her arms nor run up and down the room to try and get some warmth into her legs because the occupants of the other two beds would inform Madame about her and then the woman would gloat, knowing that her punishment had been successful. Even now after several months she could not believe what had happened to her. In a day she had been plunged from glory into a prison and it was Uncle Laurent's fault.

Why did he hate her so much? "What that child needs is discipline," but this was unjust. He had said it over and over again throughout the long Sunday afternoons when her friends were chattering gaily under the trees at the farm while she was sitting on a hard stool with her hands folded on her lap. She had never disobeyed him in words (although often in her thoughts) but he had argued day after day with her mother until she had been sent to this school, not for education as she openly declared but to learn what unhappiness was. There had been no luxuries at home but Jeannette had baked the bread and they had fetched the vegetables from their own garden. Here Madame Berthoud actually boasted that she bought the withered greens at the market which it was not worth while for the farmers to take home and they lived on watery soup. "It is only for a year," her mother had said to console her but had she counted the days in such a cycle or the hours even in a week? Besides, it was not only time. She would never see the white, springing mountain streams leap to freedom with such ecstasy again. Nor climb the hills nor count the goats. Always now, wherever she looked, there would be fear.

What did this discipline mean of which they spoke so much? It seemed to consist of immobility and silence and of never having a thought in one's head. In France, the daughters of the booksellers had carried leaflets from one revolutionary to another just as she had carried them to Mazelet and had known glory if they had sometimes been arrested on the way. If it were sinful to choose freedom, she would choose sin. The triumphant emotion she was feeling now was hatred and she would try to suppress all other feelings. There were only two things it was impossible to give up, the Revolution because it represented hope and her tutor, Monsieur Alexandre.

The two things were really part of one another. Monsieur Alexandre came twice a week to teach them grammar and history and although he had hurriedly stooped to pick it up, she had once caught sight of a scrap of green ribbon in his hand. He dared not speak of Paris but sometimes when he was talking about the struggles of the citizens in ancient wars, she knew instinctively that he was thinking about Berne. He never said, as Madame Berthoud did, "The only virtue for a woman is obedience." How could she wait a year to be free? There was only misery at school, sore throats, coughs, the incessant hunger that a beggar must feel and worst of all the sensation that time was moving on with sunsets she would never see, bright, clear mornings when she could not go with Henriette to gather berries up the hills, a whole four seasons through which she had never properly lived.

Why did her mother allow Uncle Laurent to dictate to her? She had heard what people said about him in the town. "Monsieur Perrin is more Bernois than they are themselves, it is always 'no' with him and never 'yes.'" Was it because he was angry that his brother had married a foreigner or because he imagined that she knew why Antoine had run away? Endure, people would say, but she looked from the dull, white faces of her fellow pupils back to Mazelet and she knew that nothing that might happen to her in the future could touch such an experience again.

The thin smoke of a spring bonfire was almost the color of the sky. A clump of late cowslips was spreading along the grass as Alexandre hoped the Revolution would spread from one end of Vaud to the other. It was the first day that he had smelled April in the air and if he were free he would stroll down to the lake, it was a long but favorite walk, to meet his friends, the boatmen. *"Bonjour,* Monsieur Alexandre," they would shout as he arrived, "if you have come, the good weather is here." They would offer to take him out fishing in a week or two when they had finished repairing their nets. Alas, he could not do as he wished. It was the lessons that he gave at Madame Berthoud's school that paid the rent of his room. He hated the airless place, the widow's yellow cheeks and the miserable faces of her pupils, he often wondered if she allowed them to walk in the garden even on a summer day? The dust clung to the broken threads of the worn door-mat and except for the salon, it was never entered unless there were parents to receive in it; the walls were peeling and damp. As ever, when he wanted to dream rather than think, the never ending uncertainties of life began to trouble his mind. He was staring at what he called the cockade of liberty, the snowy mountains and clusters of the vines, that the Bernois could never destroy unless they could obliterate the hills. People shouted a friendly greeting to him, a puppy, all legs, licked his hand, there was even a sail, it must be the first boat out, below him on the water. Yet there was tyranny and he would not retract the word, to make nonsense of his peaceful thoughts. He could not suppress the memory, shameful though it was, that it was here, on this path, a wide one many people used, that he had been thinking of his namesake's triumph, the great Alexander, who had held the world in his hands, and had not noticed a man advancing toward him from the opposite direction. He had barely touched him but with a blow that he had felt for days afterward, the fellow had knocked his hat off into the ditch, the very hat that he was still wearing because he could not afford to buy another. "Look where you are going, fool," the man had snarled, "haven't they taught you to bow to your superiors in your village?" It had been one of the minor tax collectors, those hated officials sent to weigh the corn of the poorest peasant so that he would pay the dues to a city he would never see while his own family was short of food. "We give you order and stability" a Bernese proclamation ran but it was a lie. Farmers or fishermen, the folk here could keep the peace themselves, they needed no master to impose laws from outside. "Down with Berne," he muttered as he climbed up the bank to look down at the shore, nature was growing at this time of the year, each part of the landscape had its color, its own movement, the old fruit trees still covered with blossom, a patch of sand, almost the shape of a butterfly, lying just clear of the lake. Why was it that mankind always wanted to change something or other and Madame Berthoud's face came into his mind. How could parents leave their children at the mercy of such a woman, especially Sophie, the newcomer? She alone seemed really interested in his stories but to survive, he noticed, she was sliding into a mute despair that might affect her for the rest of her life.

Sophie was a stranger, she had not sprung out of the soil of some Vaudois village, he was a stranger because of his learning and empty pockets. They were as mistrusted in consequence as if they were a pair of the roaming but by now legendary wolves.

"Sit up, Sophie, continue your work." The names changed, it might be Adèle or Marthe but the implacable command was always the same. Yet what was the use of this alphabet, erased, rewritten but never cherished as the letter from a friend would be or the word *"Liberté"* scribbled on a wall? The blotch on the table could not be turned into a picture, it was merely an ink stain on the dirty wood. Nor was the table solid, one leg had sunk into a slight depression in the floor, it was not enough to make it rickety but only unstable so that the line that she was forming was too thick.

There was a knock at the door and they all stood up as Monsieur Alexandre came in. His lessons were the only tolerable moments of Sophie's week. Her schoolfellows were interested in their ribbons or gossiping about their relatives but in spite of Madame Berthoud's sister who sat as watchdog in a corner, Alexandre had taught her how the mind could free itself into a mute if sometimes unnoticed defiance. The beginning was dull, he corrected their grammar and taught them the right phrases with which to begin or end a letter according to its purpose. She resented the flowery phrases people were expected to use to friends; if she ever received any correspondence she would know at once whether the writer were sympathetic or not and if it were on business a single form would suffice. "A letter is a work of art" he would remind them but she had never had any, her mother heard at long intervals from her sisters and Uncle Laurent occasionally from Antoine. It seemed a waste of time because it was only when the precious hour was almost up that he shut the book to tell them about wars and cities so ancient and far away that the names seemed to rise from a fog like the old walnut tree in November from the mist around its roots. Yet there was a king, his namesake it appeared, who had ridden towards the sunrise for almost a year. Instead of having to obey the present stupid laws, he had seen temples, hills and marvels until Sophie also floated on the words, half in a dream but also feeling the sand round her again as in those long, now forbidden days beside the lake, far from this prison to which Uncle Laurent had consigned her where the only stove was in Madame Berthoud's room and was always going out. They quickly found a new excuse as to why there was not enough firewood to get it going again. Yet she could almost forget the cold, imagining the king riding forward, forward, over the hot, dusty sand.

She started, Monsieur Alexandre had begun to question the girl at her side. "Why did the king attack the Persians?" The girl beside her who was so fond of quoting texts, merely to please Madame Berthoud, had not even been listening. Somebody else made a fumbling answer and then it was her turn. "What happened to Alexander at the end?" She was supposed to reply that penitence (as Madame Berthoud repeated) was essential although Sophie doubted if her teacher believed this himself. She yelled rather than spoke in the low whisper that they were taught to employ in class, "Alexander was a conqueror and happy. He saw the marvels of the world and died when he was young."

"Do you think he wanted to die?" She did not notice her tutor looking at her in a troubled, anxious manner.

"Of course. And I should like to die as he did. Without the Revolution what is there in life in front of me." She never noticed her fellow pupils drawing away in terror from her hardly sane but triumphant face.

"My brother-in-law commended the school and it has an excellent reputation." This visitor who had appeared so unexpectedly at her door was disturbing, Madame Perrin thought, and she wished he would leave. He must have worn the brown coat he had on for years although admittedly there was not a speck of dust on it and there was a barely concealed crack across the top of one shoe.

"The same institutions do not suit all pupils." Alexandre was noticing the threadbare carpet at his feet. It was a different shape and color from the ones in general use and he wondered if Sophie's mother had brought it from England with her?

"Sophie must learn discipline."

"Ought we not to ask first what discipline is?" He could not remember that his father had ever punished him but instead he had taught him his early lessons so well through rhymes and stories that he had always been at the top of his class.

"Surely it is a way of life. My daughter must be obedient."

Why, Alexandre was tempted to inquire but he must proceed warily, he was risking his own position at the school and, as he had reminded himself again throughout the afternoon, his post there paid his rent and with all he could say, in spite of this danger, he might still be unable to save his pupil.

"The kind of discipline she is enduring now will harden her and dull her native intelligence. Afterwards she will marry the first youth she meets just to get away from you."

"From me?" She had nursed the restless child on her knee mile after mile through the long drive through France when with each hour she had become more terrified of the strangeness of the land and of the ever increasing distance from her birthplace.

"You put her into the school. You will not even listen when she tries to tell you what it is doing to her."

"My brother-in-law would be angry if I took her away."

"Monsieur Perrin is naturally of more importance than your own daughter."

The impudence! Madame Perrin half rose, she ought to order the man to leave her house at once. Yet she had to admit that Sophie had shown a sullenness towards her recently that she had never displayed at home. "The fees are paid till the end of the year."

"Money is always more important than a mere life." Alexandre would have liked to throw the necessary coins into her lap but he had barely enough to buy an occasional fish from his boatmen friends, let alone save for his old age.

"Do you really mean she is suffering?" Madame Perrin was as afraid of Laurent as Daniel had been while he was alive. Yet it was true that Sophie had acted so strangely on her last visit that she had not been to see her recently, she pretended to herself that it was so as not to unsettle her but actually she had been afraid, she knew, of the girl's reproachful face.

"I see it is useless to discuss the matter." Alexandre was angry. How he hated the bourgeoisie. Such women wept over a drowning kitten but would not lift a finger to rescue their own children from cruelty if it meant breaking a rule of their particular group. He had risked his own position for nothing although he would have come, he supposed, whatever the outcome, just as he would have jumped into the lake in his only suit to save some stranger from drowning. "Sophie is learning the same obedience from Madame Berthoud that a captive shows to stop them from beating him again until the first stripes have healed. But who knows what a volcano is existing underneath."

"I must consult Laurent," Madame Perrin muttered the words almost to herself, "he lent me the money for the fees."

"Is he the child's father?"

"No." Oh, Daniel, she thought, but saying the name aloud would not help. Daniel had been buried years before in front of the mountains, the mountains that had won him at the end. Would he have sent his child to Madame Berthoud? She knew he would have kept his daughter at home. Let Sophie be happy, he had said suddenly, just before the fever became worse. If Daniel had disobeyed his brother and had stayed on at some little farm in Vaud, she would never have met him but he might still be alive. Laurent, Daniel, she knew to whom her loyalty was owed. "Very well, I will go and see her tomorrow and if she is as unhappy as you say, then I will bring her home."

Chapter Seven

Sophie opened her eyes. Fortunately it was still too dark to get up. To lie under the heavy quilt and dream was the one rich moment of these winter days. First there was the initiation each evening when she pulled off petticoats and stockings before leaping between the icy sheets and gradually the warmth that seemed to absorb itself inwardly, as sand dried the ink on her copy book, began to creep back into fingers and toes. Then she could think of summer, of goats nibbling the mountain pastures and streams washing back the long grasses as they rushed down the hills.

"Sophie!"

There was only a rim of forehead visible as Madame Perrin pushed open the door and looked down at the apparently sleeping figure, shading the light from the candlestick with her hand so as not to startle her daughter. One day the child would suffocate, pulling the bedclothes over her face like that! It was strange that so active and lively a girl should be so susceptible to the cold!

"Sophie!"

There was no reply. Madame Perrin bent down and jerked away the quilt. "And you call yourself a revolutionary! Can't you hear the drums? The Château has been occupied and they say Ménard and his Frenchmen are about to cross the lake."

"Must we go now?" Sophie yawned. If Vaud was free, the

world was in order, her bed was warm and nobody would celebrate before the sun was up. She tried to pull the quilt back over her legs. The cold cut like a whip.

"Come along, sluggard, I want to hear what your Uncle Laurent has to say," Madame Perrin stopped to pick up a stocking that had fallen onto the floor, "if you are not dressed within five minutes, we shall go off without you."

Sophie yawned a second time and reached for the other stocking that was hanging over a stool. She knew from experience that she would feel warmer once her legs were inside the thick wool. Only a little light was coming through the slats of the shutters but her mother had left her the candle. The strings of her petticoat knotted themselves mysteriously and she could not find the end of the ribbon she wanted, the comb caught in her tangled hair and then she had to feel along the wall before she discovered her slippers. Sluggard! Why was it supposed to be so shameful? It was hard to be a rebel thus early in the morning but she wondered how Monsieur Alexandre had felt when he had heard the news?

It was nearer ten minutes than five when she ran down the stairs to find Jeannette pouring soup into the familiar blue bowls. "We are not going out into this weather without something hot inside us," her mother passed round the bread, "but hurry, the Gerbiers have already left."

"It's too hot."

"Lace your boots up while you let it cool."

"There," Jeannette had been bending over the fire, "it's low but I've put some logs ready so we can soon warm the kitchen when we get back."

"Are you sure it's safe?" The one thing that Madame Perrin was afraid of was fire. Suppose a spark should fall on a bit of rag while they were away and she returned to find the few things she owned were cinders?

"Oh Maman! How can anything happen with the oven closed and a stone hearth?" Sophie gulped down the last of her soup and wished her mother would be sensible. Other people even left logs burning when they went out but if Uncle Laurent invited them to dinner, they climbed up to a freezing house afterwards. She put her bowl down and fastened her shawl.

"Not so fast! Where is that green cockade Monsieur Alexandre gave you? It's as unsafe to go to the Place du Marché without it this morning as it would have been to wear it a fortnight ago."

How swiftly things changed! Sophie noticed to her amazement that Jeannette and her mother had already pinned their emblems to their wraps. She dug her own ribbon from underneath her school books and Madame Perrin smiled. "What a hiding place for a conspirator! Did you never think that if I pay for your lessons it is natural to look at your exercises to see if you are making progress and your rosette would be the first thing I should find."

The cold took their breath away as soon as they left the house. It was too dark to see more than the outline of the hills but they could just manage not to stray from the roads. A single, dull beat reminded Sophie of the icicles the children struck while they waited their turn in winter at the fountain. "The drummers are out," Jeannette pulled back the flap of her bonnet to listen, "all the villagers are marching to Lausanne."

"How did you hear the news?"

"The saddler banged on our door as he passed."

A boy ran out of a garden, followed by his dog. A neighbor joined them, a thick, brown shawl tied over her head as if it were a hood, the first houses began to emerge in the growing light but the peaks were blotted out under their caps of snow.

"Look!" Sophie pointed towards the bands of men, all waving flares as they marched down the slopes, the tips of light, she thought, dissolving like drops of honey into the darkness, "Look, they've all got torches. Why do we have to go to Uncle Laurent? We can't see the celebrations from his house. Everything will happen in the square."

"It is a very anxious time for him and he will expect us to call. The neighbors know he has always been loyal to Berne though really what he wanted was stability and peace." Daniel had been careful never to criticize but he had spoken of the natural unity of the towns along the lake and Madame Perrin knew he would have stood beside her at the bonfire today had he still been alive. She looked at Sophie's excited face and wondered why the girl could not realize that she held her tongue from prudence rather than conviction. They were foreigners and as such it was wiser to be silent.

The gate was closed when they came to Jean Michel's house. Even now, as Sophie looked up sadly at the shutters, it was as if the one triumphant moment of her life had been wiped out. It would always be in two halves; the time before she was sent to Madame Berthoud and the days since she had left that school. She longed to defy her mother, to hurl herself against the locked door, shouting *Liberté, Egalité,* but the place was empty. No doubt a rumor had reached the *vigneron* the previous evening and with his wife he had gone down to spend the night with Mazelet. Yet what could the celebrations mean to Marie? Freedom had come too late to save her son from death on a foreign battlefield.

Fishermen came up the little paths between the black winter stocks of the vines, women waited for a group to pass and then joined it, the people now were marching in compact bands. "It's useless your going with me to see your uncle," Madame Perrin was suddenly indulgent, "take the girl to the

Place du Marché, Jeannette, but don't stay there too long. I shall not wait for the bonfire this evening so come to Monsieur Perrin's house early. I want to get home before dark."

A huge green banner was floating above the Palud but they could not push their way into the little square, it was already full of shouting citizens. Sophie could just see the flag and the head of the figure of Justice above the fountain from the slope where she was standing with Jeannette. It had taken them more than an hour, greeting friends and lingering on the way, to reach the center of the city.

"Brothers, Citizens . . . ," the rest of the speech was lost as a dozen farmers surged forward, their heavy boots resounding on the pavement like a recruiting sergeant's drum, with so many students and apprentices behind them that people were clinging to the arms of complete strangers to keep themselves upright.

"Liberty for us all!" It did not matter to Sophie that her voice was lost in the uproar, nobody could reprove her for being noisy today. It was not just wearing a cockade, this was the opening of the gates. Liberty meant freedom for the women as well as the men to learn, talk, ride, just as Antoine had done and she wondered where he was at this moment? When would he hear the news? Perhaps not till the spring when he picked up a gazette at some coffee house or in a letter from a merchant in Holland whose name they did not even know. She would not despise a counting house as he had done. It would be more exciting to write out items in a ledger, ten sacks of coffee, a packet of nutmeg or cinnamon or to enter the arrival of a ship than to fold up sheets for a lifetime and put them in a press and hear the news when it was stale because of cooking the supper.

"No more tithes!" The farmers were shouting so vigorously

that they overwhelmed the distant yells of "Liberty and Vaud." A boy shoved in front of them with a cudgel under his arm and a faded gray patch under the collar of his tattered brown coat. A man shifted a child to his other shoulder, people linked arms. "I always wanted a blue cup," an old countrywoman put her hand on Jeannette's shoulder to steady herself as if Jeannette were her dearest friend, "and now, if it's really true that we can keep the money from the corn instead of paying most of it to the landlord, perhaps I can buy one."

"And then you'll be afraid that somebody will break or steal it," a peasant shouted behind her, the insecurely fastened cockade in his felt hat bobbing up and down above his red cheeks. His clothes smelled of wine when they turned round to look at him.

"I want it if only for a day," and the people round them laughed.

"Salut!" Jeannette recognized Suzanne, the apple woman, at the end of the row, "What a day this is for us!"

"We've waited long enough!"

The crowd was moving in two ways. One half was struggling downhill to the speeches at the Palud and the other half was heaving itself upward toward Montbenon to get good places for the lighting of the bonfire. Everybody Sophie knew seemed to be near, Jean Michel actually waved to her but she could not force her way through the people to get up to him. Then, as they got nearer the church, she saw her tutor, his hat pushed back on his head as if he were a boy, standing against a door. "Liberty, Monsieur Alexandre, Liberty!" He smiled as he recognized the cockade that he had given her.

"Égalité, Vaud!" It was as if by repeating the words they would be happy ever afterward. "I looked out for you,

Sophie," her tutor shouted, "but in this multitude I did not know where to find you."

"We got caught halfway down the street, you cannot get as far as the Palud, but I knew you would be here somewhere."

"Oh, it's freedom at last." Everyone would learn to read and as he tried to stand upright with the multitude surging about him, Alexandre remembered the day he had begun the alphabet, sitting on a high wooden stool with his legs still too short to reach the ground. "I am putting the riches of the world into your hands." He would never forget that sentence of his father even if it had been perhaps a little exaggerated. There were people who were afraid of books, and learning had brought him neither a thick coat nor a roast fowl though it had brought him happiness. If they had facts in daily life instead of rumors and he glanced round at the market women, the tailor's boy and the laughing, yelling apprentices, people would not obey the mere whims of an arrogant official and everybody would have a fire and a home.

"Peace! Peace!"

"And what will that bring us?" The voice of the cake seller boomed above the throng, "We shall still have to collect sticks and sweep the floors."

"Don't make me hungry!" the apple woman yelled.

"Do you remember the ginger cakes that the peddlers used to bring round on feastdays? Now it's so long since I saw any, I can't remember if they were oblong or round."

"The aristocrats gobble them up at the *Lion d'Or.*"

"There will be schools for all," Alexandre shouted, "and that is the real equality." He tried not to think of what young Guilléron had once said to him. "Have you thought what they will read, Alexandre? The latest scandals that were better forgotten, not your Roman history."

A group pushed its way to the front, they were in rags, with not a whole garment between them and their filthy, matted hair smelled of a never cleaned stable. "The fields belong to us, the fields belong to us," they chanted in a *patois* that became an unintelligible roar, "now the Bears can poison themselves with their potatoes."

"What does liberty mean to them," the man standing next Sophie muttered, "all they want is plunder."

"Égalité! Vaud!" Monsieur Alexandre got swept away toward the middle of the square but he was tall and could wave to them above the hoods, shawls and caps. "You can't linger," Jeannette said severely as Sophie tried to wriggle her way toward him, "we are late now, your mother must be wondering what has happened to us and how we are ever going to get out of this crowd, I cannot imagine."

A fire was burning inside the stove, and perhaps out of despair Laurent kept opening the door and pushing in another log while the first one was only half burned. It was good to be indoors out of the cold. Yet the house seemed lonelier than ever; *"morne"* the neighbors would have said, not mournful but desolate and drained of life. The two of them seemed lost in the great room. "What is going to happen to us?" A rebellion might mean a levy and her resources were meager. Suppose the peasants took the patch of vineyard that had belonged to Daniel and that then Laurent who looked after it could not continue her allowance, how would she be able to live and educate Sophie?

"I know no more than you do."

"Is it because of the tithes?"

"There have been abuses on some estates, I admit, but supposing the harvest is bad? The peasants have no savings to tide them over to the following summer and I have known landowners who supported the village next to them for a year."

"So now there will be more suffering and unrest?"

"What is worse is that there are French troops facing us the length of the lake. People have reported seeing bivouac fires on the opposite shore from Villeneuve to Geneva."

"Are they going to invade us?"

"Why not? We have broken our oath to Berne and are entirely defenseless."

"Tell me, I would rather know the worst, will they attack Lausanne?" The handkerchief that she had twisted till it was merely a rag, slipped to the floor and Madame Perrin bent down to pick it up. A thread was broken, she noticed, at the edge of the carpet.

"I doubt it. The revolutionary party has so completely taken power that our citizens will march toward the French with what they call a fraternal kiss. Of course our grain and wine will be seized and I suppose the soldiers will be billeted on us. I cannot go out today because I refuse to wear a cockade but I shall buy all the flour I can find tomorrow and hide it. I advise you to do the same."

"There are so many rumors, what is one to believe?" How could she take precautions if her reserves were five *écus* tied up in an old stocking and hidden in a crevice behind a cupboard?

"We have lived under Bernese rule for centuries at the price of some taxes, I admit they were high, and a little homage. It is true we had to send most of our younger sons abroad but it avoided conflicts between brothers and many of them came back eventually and were able to buy themselves houses and vineyards. Now a fever had got into our youth . . . ," he paused, he was evidently thinking about Antoine, "and it has spread to citizens who ought to have had enough experience to be governed by Reason."

"I was amazed at the crowd as we came down the hill. There were gentlemen as well as peasants."

"There are always more fools than responsible citizens. You should be far enough away from Lausanne to be safe. They are unlikely to quarter soldiers in a house occupied only by three women. But here . . . ," he looked round the room into which only a tiny circle of his friends was ever admitted, shrugged his shoulders, and sighed.

Safe? But suppose there was no food? Life had seemed difficult up to this moment, now it seemed hopeless. Yet Sophie would burst in soon, full of an ill-concealed enthusiasm that would upset her uncle and, if reproved, would sulk during the long walk home. Why would her daughter never understand that her mother was really on her side, nobody could approve of Berne's policy in keeping the peasants ignorant so as to control them more easily, but her uncle's opinions had also to be respected. He felt his son's absence very much.

"I am thankful for one thing," Laurent got up slowly, today of all days he wanted to avoid the appearance of hurry, and went over to his desk. He took out his key but, as if he were listening first for footsteps, appeared deliberately to delay opening the drawer. Finally he unlocked it, took out an envelope and returned to his chair. "Occasionally a disaster turns out to have been an advantage. This is a letter from Antoine. I am thankful now that the boy is in England and not implicated in our troubles. He seems to be doing well with that merchant to whom my cousin recommended him. Perhaps if we ever regain our senses, in a year or two he can come home."

"I am so glad you got the letter. These events will certainly delay the post." Yet would Antoine ever want to leave a great city and his personal freedom for the restrictions of a greatly impoverished Lausanne? She looked down at the carpet again, it was a pity that she had no suitable needle with her to take the necessary stitch in it. That border would fray badly unless it were quickly mended.

"Yes, I was lucky that it came. A merchant took it as far as Geneva and then a friend brought it to Monsieur Guilléron one day when he was at Morges. He carried it on to me. One week later and it would undoubtedly have been lost."

Madame Perrin longed to take the envelope out of Laurent's hand. It was stupid of her but the address had been written while it was lying on an English table and it was so long now since she had heard from her sisters. For some reason that she could not explain, how strange the processes of memory were, she thought suddenly of their neighbor, Mr. Thomas, who had lived in the opposite house to them when they were children. She supposed she had not said more than a dozen sentences to him in her life, apart from wishing him good morning, but he had seen them across the flooded road in the winter gales and sometimes given them roses from his garden. She had been so secure in England. Secure? She wondered what Sophie was doing, yelling her head off, no doubt, among the crowd, with no real knowledge of what was actually going on but simply involved in her own revolutionary dream. It was different and frightening after her own safe childhood. Laurent opened the letter, he was preparing to read it aloud and she wondered if she could bear it? It would bring home and family too vividly into her mind. Unhappily there were no straight lines in life, it was not like the ruled ledgers that lay open upon a desk. Even Daniel had been unable or unwilling to explain to her the difficulties of assimilation, the trifles, the differences here, the need for endurance there, that would assume gigantic shapes until nothing was instinctive any longer but had to be studied, word by word, action by action, as rigorously as any lesson. Sophie, who should have been her guide, had almost become her enemy, as if her own inward rebellion had flowered in her daughter. She could not even talk intimately to her any longer. Yet supposing, this was something that she must not let herself even imagine, supposing that she could return to Hastings and the seagulls perching on the roofs, their feathers the gray white of a ruffled sea, would Sophie be as awkward in that unfamiliar town as she, herself, had felt here? Perhaps not while the girl was so young and eager for fresh experiences. Besides, Sophie's attitude toward a new country would not be complicated, as in her own case, by love.

"The business details will not interest you but my son who could never tell one vine from another, seems to have satisfied his employers in England. I was gratified to hear that they have already increased his salary."

"Oh, this must reassure you as to his future."

"Yes, it is satisfying but if it had not been for that foolish escapade, he could have had the same position here with my friend, the notary, at Morges."

Madame Perrin made no reply. She was sorry for Laurent but she understood Antoine. A youth needed to prove that he could be successful by himself and not because he had a father or a relative behind him.

"It is the ferment here that is to blame. Berne is not a city to these boys, it is a father with many sons. Each one wants to go his own way and look where they have landed us! Inside the arms of the unprincipled French. Still this is not what I was anxious to tell you. Antoine has traced your sisters. They have moved from Hastings to a town some distance away where, they wrote him, the winters were milder. Both were well and grateful for news. They said it was two years since they had heard from you."

"Yet I have written them regularly, every six months." It was all that she had been able to afford.

"I know, I arranged for the forwarding of some of the letters myself."

Madame Perrin could not keep the tears out of her eyes and she was thankful that Sophie was not there to see them. Now the gulf was wider than from Ouchy to the Savoyard shore and there would be no memory with which to cross it. Her old bedroom at Hastings had been so clearly in her mind that sometimes she had felt that if she put out her hand she would feel the patchwork quilt and the walnut top of the little table beside it. Now this would fade because although remembrance did lessen as some said, it had its moments, sometimes clear, sometimes extinguished as if by fog through which one heard a muffled voice without seeing the speaker. The unseen house in which her sisters lived must always be a blank to her.

"I have their address." Laurent recalled in this moment of chaos that although he had disapproved of the marriage, Daniel's widow, unlike her unruly daughter, had never given him an instant's anxiety. "When you reply, let me enclose the letter in one that I am writing to my son. A missive to a business house has more chance of reaching its destination."

"I should be so grateful." She had much to thank Laurent for even if she sometimes dreaded his invitations. They could have been moments of quietness and warmth but Sophie always broke them up through her restlessness. Then, as if instinctively she had chosen just this moment, her daughter burst into the room, her cheeks red from the cold and her cockade pinned brazenly to the middle of her shawl. "They are lighting the beacon on Montbenon in half an hour, please, please, may Jeannette take me up to it."

Chapter Eight

"The times!" Madame Gerbier held up an unfinished mitten to measure it against its fellow, "I never thought to live through a year like this." Sophie grinned at Henriette and lifted an edge of her apron to disclose an edge of green ribbon. She was spending a day at the farm because her mother seemed more worried and readier to scold her than usual. "It's like the end of the world."

"Like! It *is* the end of the world." The farmer came unexpectedly through the door and sat down heavily in the chair near the hearth.

"I thought you were going to see Guillaume at Ouchy."

"I have seen him. I went off as you know to try to get a few more logs because Dupuy disappointed us in November by only sending up a load and a half and I thought Guillaume might tell me of a place where there were some for sale. The roads were awful, thick snow over heavy ruts. It puzzles me why my brother-in-law lives down there; it's true he's a fisherman but stopping in that damp place with nothing to look at but water, would kill me off in a month. I often wonder why my sister married him."

"Perhaps she wanted to get away from a farm. Not everyone likes thawing animals out in the kitchen."

"And because life is so dull for us," Sophie murmured very,

very softly, "wash, cook, sew, from the time we get up till we fall asleep. But the Revolution will help us, it must."

Henriette frowned and glanced round anxiously to see if Sophie had been overheard. Everything seemed in order, the farmer had taken off his heavy boots and put them to dry by the door after pulling on some dry stockings. Madame Gerbier got up to stir the soup and a door banged somewhere in the yard.

"My sister told me Guillaume had gone down to look at his boat. It's in a shelter for the winter. 'Surely not,' I said, 'in this weather.' I had been cracking tiny icicles off the branches with my thumb all the way down to the lake. 'That's where he is, if you want to talk to him.' She wasn't gay as she usually is, she seemed more anxious."

"It's lonely for her there in the winter." Madame Gerbier took up her knitting again, she was finishing a pair of extra heavy mittens for Henriette.

"Well, I went off to the shore and there he was, staring at the lake and so absorbed he never heard me come up behind him. '*Salut,* Guillaume,' I said and how he jumped! I might have been a mastiff. He seemed pleased though when he saw who I was. 'It's those barges. Are they really flying the French flag? There, out there, a little to the left of you and more than midway across the lake.'

"Ménard's come to take a bite out of us.

" 'What shall I do? Oh, what shall I do? I'm ruined if they seize my boat.'

"Do? There's nothing you can do except shout *Vive la France*. But oh, Guillaume, what have you done with your cockade? If they land, that bit of green will be as good today as a passport. Do you know he was trembling all over, yet I've seen him out in a hurricane as calm as a block of ice."

"You would scream if they threatened to take your wagon." Madame Gerbier put down her work again to thrust some sticks on the fire, "What happened then? Is Guillaume's boat safe?"

"Happened! We watched a barge coming closer and closer and when it grounded, it's shallower than it looks down there, twenty soldiers jumped ashore, waving their muskets and yelling. Their sergeant asked me most politely the way to Lausanne and I inquired if he wanted a guide."

"Oh, Henri, they might have shot you."

"There was no danger." Now it was over, Gerbier was not going to admit how much he had trembled when the men had landed.

"The French!" Sophie had been taught never to question her elders but today her curiosity was too much for her. "Do tell us what they were like."

"Not like the pictures in the *Almanach*. There were no officers in white breeches with tricolor scarves. Animals, I would have said, rather than men with great mats of hair hanging over their collars, tattered clothes and boots tied up with string. If I had met them out in a field I should have said they were fugitives from a skirmish where they had lost their equipment. But they can yell, you should have heard them yell, or maybe it was supposed to be a song."

"Did you actually lead them up to Lausanne?" Madame Gerbier looked anxious and Sophie knew what she was thinking; it could be dangerous for the farmer after the French left the city, if it were proved he had been their guide.

"No, they had been ordered to wait for the other boats so eventually I slipped away." He did not mention that he had waited for an opportunity to dodge between the huts and dash up the hill as fast as he could run. "The sergeant told Guillaume his boat was safe. They had no quarrel with us."

"Are they going to occupy Lausanne?" It was Henriette this time who dared to question her father.

"Yes, and I see no reason why our aristocrats should not make the acquaintance of the army's fleas. The sergeant said they expected to be quartered in the town. There is bound to be a levy on our money and our goods and just as soon as I have warmed myself I am going to look round the barn because we shall have to hide as much as we can of our supplies. The only difficulty will be the cattle. It's too cold at present to drive them up into the hills."

The snowflakes clinging like flowers to the bushes that bordered the garden made Sophie long all the more ardently for spring. "Distance is more important than Time," her mother said dreamily and startling though the statement sounded, it was true. They had been cut off from Lausanne for weeks by the jagged ice on the roads, Laurent seemed as far away as Antoine in London, the only difference in the dirty white of the landscape was a dark furrow under the vines and lower, just in front of Jean Michel's house, a patch of gold willows was visible, on account of its color, far below them along the lake. Everything ought to have been gay but the good times had not come. Life went on as it had before the Revolution or was even worse. The prices rose, there was no flour to be found, they had to pay double for a basket of sour apples and a cabbage. The women in the village said, *"Salut, citoyenne,"* instead of *"Salut, madame"* but it was merely a change of words. Little had altered under the surface in spite of the bonfires and the trees of liberty except that they were all a little poorer. It was winter with its chilblains and discomforts, old and young had coughs and the simplest remedies disappeared from the apothecary's shelf. As they muttered, news was the only thing available from the empty market stalls. People spoke of skirmishes in front of Berne, of groups demanding liberty in far away Soleure. This was not the great rebellion that Sophie had imagined, an event to make her equal with Antoine and able to enter a counting house herself.

Freedom, people grumbled, was a luxury that they could not afford. The French had to be fed, they asked for men to join the militia, wine had almost disappeared. The landowners, most of whom were secretly loyal to Berne, naturally had to pay the heaviest dues but the artisans who had shouted loudest at the bonfires also grumbled that their faded emblems were all they had to show for their pains. February passed, March began and one morning Sophie was able to go out with a pointed stick to test the ground for the spring sowing. Was it imagination? The lake seemed to have grown shallower although melting snow and rain ought to have increased its volume. It was only in July that the water receded and left edges of yellow sand around the rocks. "The birds," her mother said, she had followed her daughter with a basket; "now I believe the winter is over. But what does the farmer want, I wonder, look, he is coming towards us, waving his arms, he must have news."

Gerbier was so excited that he forgot the customary salutations, "Hurry, get your shawls and come. The French have won a battle in front of Berne and have entered the city. They are building bonfires on all the hills of Vaud to celebrate our victory. Come with us to Montbenon."

"How did you hear?"

"The news passed from village to village and Jean Michel, he happened to be spending the night in Lausanne, rushed up to tell us."

"What will happen now? Will it mean more taxes?" Madame Perrin looked as troubled as if Gerbier were warning them that the Bernese army was marching on the city. How could her mother be so unimaginative? The tyranny was over and that was all that mattered. *"Vive la Liberté,"* Sophie shouted at the top of her voice.

"Be quiet, Sophie, we can express our assent without screaming." Her daughter's exuberance had been the most difficult to bear of all Madame Perrin's winter trials. Yet Daniel would have been on the side of the insurgents, it was Berne that had exiled him for seven years from the mountains he so loved.

"There will be another levy and I paid enough in February besides having my best herdsman leave to join the militia. I hope he's safe. I don't know what I shall do in April if he doesn't return. But it would have been far worse if Berne had been able to reimpose her rule. I might have lost my farm and it looked as if her intrigues would be successful as late as last month."

"You think we shall be safe?" Laurent had been careful but his neutrality now would be counted as a sign that he had secretly favored Berne and without his help and his management of the small vineyard Daniel had left her, how would they live?

"Safe?" Gerbier shrugged his shoulders, "as safe as we ever are. I may own the best pair of oxen in the country and lose them in an avalanche on the summer pasture. All we actually know is that there was a battle and the French then occupied Berne. Now the aristocrats will learn the subjection that they have made us feel for years. But nobody is going to tell me when to plant my land again nor take half of my harvest in dues."

"We've won," Sophie shouted, tugging at her mother's dress, "we've won." She forgot that it was the French who had gained the victory.

"Get your shawl, Madame Perrin, or if, as my wife does,

you fear the walk, let Sophie come with me and Henriette. I left the girl looking for her cloak but she will be waiting on the road for us. We can't be late getting back, I have to feed the cattle."

Sophie stood in terror for a moment, watching her mother's face. It would be like her with her fears of causing Uncle Laurent distress, to forbid her to go to the city. "Oh, she would follow you, Monsieur Gerbier, whether I said yes or no today. Hurry and put on your other dress, Sophie, don't scream too loudly and, above all, be obedient."

Chapter Nine

1800

How could he have imagined in the calm world of his youth that its values could dissolve in a day? Laurent stared at the carpet in front of him, it was familiar but old, he wanted to renew it but his friends were being ruined one by one, he had had to sell his best vineyard to pay the new levy and, except that it showed a man who his enemies were, he would have liked to tear off and trample on every green cockade he saw. The taxes had always been heavy, he agreed that Berne had demanded more than the poorer villages could afford, yet look at the stability the city had given them in return! He was even thankful now that his son was in a foreign land, away from Lausanne where family was ranged against family and where the old, beautiful order of relationships had completely broken down.

"The separation from your daughter will be hard," how gray his face seemed when he caught sight of it in the mirror, "but Mrs. Peterson is English."

As if that made a difference! It was simply a label. Madame Perrin stared at the square of blue sky between the trees that she could see through the opposite window and wondered what Mrs. Peterson would be like as a mistress?

"It is a wonderful opportunity for you." He had dreaded the interview and in his embarrassment Laurent began to count silently the painted roses on the cabinet door, it was a trick he had when he was worried.

"I must think her offer over."

"It would be an act of incredible folly to refuse."

Laurent was hard, always had been hard, and he resented not being able to fit her daughter into the acceptable Vaudois mold. "But Sophie needs my care. That school you advised was a disaster." She had lost through it, she knew, Sophie's devotion forever.

"If the girl will promise to be obedient, she can stay with me here."

"No," the discipline would drive her daughter into some foolish entanglement just to escape from it. "It's very kind of you but I think," she stared at the painted roses herself, trying to find an excuse and, like a flash of summer lightning, one came to her, "she is better in the country. The Gerbiers have a girl her own age and they asked me yesterday if I would let Sophie go with Henriette for a few weeks to their relatives in the hills to help over the harvest."

"Would she be happy with the Gerbiers?" Laurent knew, and was secretly ashamed of it, that he could not put up with the girl's impetuousness for long in his own house yet he did not like the idea of his niece growing up on a farm. He would not have left Antoine there although the farmer was honest and never wore, he had noticed, a cockade.

"She has Henriette and at that age they need companionship but I must think the situation over and all that it means to me! Remember, I should have to give up my home." She had Sophie's lust for freedom almost as badly as her daughter and she wondered if she could bear being confined to a small apartment and never going out except on some dull errand? Mrs. Peterson might speak of needing a companion because she did not speak a word of French but what she really wanted was a servant.

If he could only tell his sister-in-law that he would make her a bigger allowance to meet the rising prices, this unpleasant interview could end. Yet he did not even know if he could pay her the quarterly sum she expected even for another three months. He was using up his reserves and eating less than his own servants so as to try to save the family house for his son.

"If I could only return to my sisters!" Madame Perrin's own savings were almost exhausted and food cost more every week. How well she understood people who said they did not want to live.

"But that is exactly what the Petersons have promised. Directly there is an opportunity for them to return to their home, they will include you and your daughter in their party."

"But when will the war end?" The gazettes were full of rumors that never came true. "It would be an exchange, I suppose, I should go back to my family and Antoine would return to you."

"I miss him but he is safer in London as long as the French are plundering us. At least he likes his work there." Laurent strolled over to the small window, adjusted a curtain and came back to his chair. "Do you suppose that surly boy, Masson I think his name was, had anything to do with Antoine's foolishness? I sent him to Monsieur Guilléron after he was fished out of the lake. If so, it was a cruel way to repay me."

"I never even heard Antoine speak of him, can he have known him?"

"They must have seen each other, Masson was sent over so often with messages. I miss Guilléron very much, we had been at the College together and if it had not been for the cold last winter and all our anxieties, I am sure he would still be alive. Fortunately I can trust his son although he has not got his father's experience."

Yet perhaps young Guilléron, Madame Perrin knew and liked him, was better adapted to the times than his old father. Masson was a vague shadow in her mind, all she could recall of him was meeting a youth on the doorstep with a package, in clothes that seemed perpetually too small for him. "Surely a boy like that could never have influenced your son?"

"Sometimes we fall under the spell of the oddest creatures. Still the College, as I found out too late, was full of dangerous ideas and I suppose Antoine was led astray by his schoolfellows. Liberty! What did those children know about it? Or what it would bring us here. French troops crossing the mountains, being greeted by idiotic women with flowers and then demanding our forage, our linen, and our stores. What those young fools were rebelling against was discipline."

"Yes," Madame Perrin nodded, under no circumstances was she going to contradict her brother-in-law but excessive severity, when it was not tempered by kindness, as it was in Laurent's case, naturally made them rebel.

"Mrs. Peterson has promised that you can have a day a month to spend with your daughter. Gerbier can bring her with him when he comes down to the market and I will see that you have a room here where you can be together."

"I cannot understand why I never hear now from my sisters." Her mind was fixed on her birthplace as though it were a talisman that could protect her from the future.

"We live with uncertainty but how can it be otherwise when there is no difference any longer." Laurent missed the outward tokens of respect, the peasants taking off their caps to him when he rode up to his vineyard (but it was not his land any longer) to inspect the vines and discuss the probable quality of the wine. He was ashamed of being unable to help his sister-in-law and her patience made him all the more irritable. "They say the Bernese were harsh but they were not severe enough. When I think of those ridiculous trees of liberty . . . ," he brought his fist so angrily down on the table beside him that a heap of papers were scattered over the floor; then, as if ashamed of his violence, he added more gently, "let me tell Mrs. Peterson that you will accept the offer. The fighting cannot go on very much longer and you can return with them to your home."

"You must remember, Sophie, we have no savings left."

"I can work at the farm, I know more than Henriette about goats, she knows more about vines."

"No." It was the sharp tone her mother always used if she were forbidding her daughter some pleasure. "If your uncle is able to sell this house, there will be enough to pay for your board. Madame Gerbier is asking very little for you but I have promised you will try to teach Henriette some of the lessons that you learned at school."

"They won't be any use to her."

"Obedience is still a virtue, Sophie, however much you despise it." Yet Madame Perrin could not speak with conviction because underneath the surface she agreed with her daughter. When would Henriette need more learning than to write down the number of litres of milk or the baskets of apples that she sold, and the only two books she would read would be the Bible and the *Almanach*. "Monsieur Gerbier is going to bring you with him when he comes to Lausanne and once a month we shall have a day together."

"Only one day? And for how long?"

"Till the war ends. The Petersons want to return to England as soon as they can get away and have offered to take us with them."

So there was a purpose behind this sudden decision and it was not due, as Sophie had supposed, entirely to Uncle Laurent's meanness. Her roots were here but it would be exciting to have the adventure of the journey and to live in a new country for a time.

"You see, it is not going to be so difficult." Madame Perrin had noticed the expression in Sophie's face.

"They say the English never keep their word."

"Haven't I kept my word to you?"

"But you are almost Vaudois."

"Almost? I thought I was so completely once." Yet Daniel's face had become indistinct although she had supposed she could never forget a line of it. He had become a shadow behind memory, bright for an instant only if she heard his name or saw a man holding a bridle in the familiar way, close to the neck of a horse.

"I shall need a new apron." Both of her own were ink stained and that made Sophie remember school. "Can I say goodbye to Monsieur Alexandre? I should like to thank him for being so kind to me."

"It won't be necessary. You must not forget what he has taught you, and Uncle Laurent has agreed that you can take a lesson with him the day you come to Lausanne. Your uncle is paying for them so remember to thank him when you see him next."

"Couldn't we move to Lausanne and then you could come home every evening."

"No, that is the time when Mrs. Peterson may need me, besides the rents are higher and as for my finding other work, in these unsettled times, there are three people after every post. But first you are going to the mountains with Henriette and if you are going to herd the goats with her, you will need a new pair of boots and a straw hat."

It was strange that the most beautiful day was often broken by some disturbing thought. When they were up on the hills Sophie often forgot her mother for hours at a time and then felt guilty when she remembered her at night. These slopes with the short, bright grass and the clouds leaping like long, white animals over the peaks were where she belonged and she felt an unreasonable contempt for all who did not agree with her. She longed to follow the stream that cut its way through the overhanging grasses to curve round a rock and disappear to where or what she did not know. Freedom was the basis of being, it need not cost a batz, and yet most people seemed to push it away from them. The only real enemy was winter and the snow. She liked to ramble but today she had to watch the goats. The big white one usually nibbled in the same place but the three small grays preferred to disappear and at this hour of the day, they blurred into the dark shadows beneath the rocks. As for the yellowish brown that tried to nip her whenever she passed close to it, not even Henriette could discover the spots where it perched. They said the sweetest grass was on a precipice and no doubt it was easier to balance on four legs than on two but the extraordinary thing about the herd was that at the precise moment when the sun began to sink, the animals formed up like soldiers on a march, ready to descend to be milked.

"Count them, Sophie, count them." It was a task they usually shared but today Henriette had been sent off with bread to those haymakers who were also clinging to tiny patches of the much valued mountain grass and she would not be back for another hour. It was the best moment of the summer, sitting here in nailed boots and a dirty overall cut from the same stuff that Madame Gerbier used for her husband's working shirts but she hated having her attention distracted from the mountains of which her mother was so much afraid, by the growing anxiety that one of the wretched creatures that she was supposed to be herding, might fall off a boulder or wander away.

Far below there was a smudge of the yellow globe flowers that grew on damp ground. She could see the cream-colored patches on the cows in the pasture, their tails beating a war against the flies. Here she was alive, in towns people merely existed, doing the same things season after season until all their vitality died. Her mistake had been to suppose that once the domination of Berne was broken, they would be completely free. The tyranny had not been destroyed, it had merely gone underground, the old forms pushed the new ones continually, if secretly, aside. Jean Michel had said that the Republic had failed in France because of the dictatorship but how much did he really know? Nor did the conflict seem to be simply between the young and the old, Uncle Laurent would have voted for order as a youth, Monsieur Alexandre would always have been a rebel. But Liberty? She ground the nails of her boots against the rock until it was pitted with white dots. How could she go on listening for eleven months of the year to women chattering about embroidery stitches or some new recipe for a cake? There was something older than this complacency, this craving for roots (who wanted roots?) and she knew she was like the stream, crashing down the mountainside, to look for the wide, adventuring river. If they guessed the thoughts that were ringing through what they called her empty head, they would punish her as Madame Berthoud had done at school, but nothing they did would change her.

"One," she began again, the white goat was placid and

never moved far from its chosen bit of grass. "Two, three, four," the animals were actually visible in a zigzag line on a slope, "five," where was the yellow one, it seemed to have disappeared, all she could see was a slab of empty rock.

"It's all right, I counted them on the way up," Henriette dropped down beside her with an empty basket dangling from her arm, "it's hot, but we must start down earlier this evening, I found a magnificent patch of bilberry bushes because I came up a new path. They are at their best, full of juice and they've had the sun on them but they won't be so good tomorrow. We must pick a hatful each before we go down to supper."

Chapter Ten

Autumn, 1801

"*Au revoir,* Alexandre! We shall not see you again, I suppose, before the spring."

"Won't you be coming to Lausanne for the St. Martin?"

"Perhaps, perhaps, it depends upon what happens."

"How mild it is for October." The firs were still their dusty, summer green and there were even a few roses left on some of the bushes. It was only here and there in the more exposed fields that a leaf or two was drifting along the grass. "It makes me forget about winter."

"I'm thankful we had good weather for the *vendanges.* I thought it might have rained."

It was the countryman who was the real pessimist, not the philosopher. A warmer than usual day was a sign that the plants would be cut down by frost and a sunny April that spring would be followed by a drought. "But I thought the price was good this year, cousin?"

"It has to be, Alexandre, if we are to live. What I ask myself is, why did they make all those changes? First they abolish the tithes, and in this they were just to us, but then the landowners get themselves elected to the Council and impose them again and what's worse, demand the arrears shall be paid as well. What does it matter to me whether they meet at Lausanne or Berne? These gentlemen in their silk stockings and white shirts never have to dig or prune or clamber up and down the slopes as we do. Why should we pay tithes to them when they do nothing for us? You've carried a hod up the hill yourself, did you enjoy it?"

"It takes the Republic time to settle down." Yet Alexandre had to admit that in the almost three years since they had lit the bonfire on Montbenon, the people were poorer and hungrier than ever. While one faction intrigued against another, the landowners were quietly regaining their power. Some of the revolutionaries had even been arrested and it was so confusing that he was even puzzled himself.

"The Republic! Why couldn't the fools have left things alone? I see no reason why I should pay taxes to Berne when I have never seen nor want to see that city. But now everything I buy costs more, the stakes for the vines are double what they were last year and all this talk about rights hasn't stopped our aristocrats from claiming their dues. It's arguments, arguments, while things go from bad to worse. But I must not keep you, cousin, if you want to reach Lausanne before dark. Thanks for all your help with the grapes."

Alexandre despised himself for not daring to continue the argument but they had fed and sheltered him for a month and it was the only place where, presuming on a somewhat distant kinship, he could escape from the cares of the city for a while. Liberty! The word was like those last red roses climbing over the wall but it seemed to have little practical effect upon their lives. The citizens were naturally impatient and he had not contradicted them when they had complained about the behavior of the French soldiers, because he had been jostled against the wall by them himself. He doubted if one of their officers had read the *Encyclopedia,* he feared that they had never heard of it nor of the chances it offered to the intellect of Man. It was the ordinary changes in their daily lives that seemed to need years. Extraordinary ones such as the proclamation of their freedom either never happened at all or came in a day. He had expected people to help each other, for prices to fall and for every citizen to find work. "Consider, then act," he had preached to his pupils since his boyhood but nobody listened to him. He knew his cousin would rather return to Bernese rule and a certain market for his grapes than bear what could be only a few transitional years of hardship. It was cowardly not to protest but even a philosopher, and he had been a follower of Diderot since his youth, had to eat. "Now you will be able to keep your sons at home," he had said that noon to his cousin's wife over their soup, the French would need recruits no longer for their army if there were peace. "To starve, I suppose," she had answered him angrily and had not offered him a second slice of bread.

"Till the St. Martin, cousin." He picked up the small bundle of his possessions and started off at a good pace down the hill. Perhaps no individual was true to his beliefs? Life was passing and what had he gained from it? Learning, yes, but from want of use how much had already vanished out of his head. In the old days (was he also regretting them?) people had seemed more generous. Why had he never had the courage then to buy a stick, walk into France, see their bookshops and hear, perhaps, some of their scientists talk? It would have been the opening to him of a second world. But how would he have got a passport, another part of his mind had argued, or been able to convince the officials that he needed to make the journey? That was the trouble of having a brain, one thought things out to a logical conclusion. Ought he . . . ought he . . . but what could he do now to escape from his ever growing poverty? People had to pay the levy, part of their stores were requisitioned, then they could not afford extra lessons for their children. Madame Berthoud had reduced his visits from three to one a week and the assistance that he had been giving to a merchant's son to help him with his calligraphy would end in another month. What would become of him during the winter? He must refuse to think about it (only what else could he do if he woke up while it was still dark) he had been lucky, he had helped to pick the grapes and his cousin had kept him for a whole month on the farm. The air was crisp, the clouds were a soft, romantic gray, far below him he could just see the ring of white sand where he had bathed as a boy. Yes, he had known liberty if all his supper had been a single crust of bread. His studies had freed him from the peasants' superstitions and even the scarcity of books had made him think over each sentence until it made as many rings in his head as his hand in the water when he dipped it into the lake. He smiled now over his passionate rebellions. The more he absorbed this moment, this last instant of the pale gold colors of straw and leaf and earth before the snow, the more he let the pure exhilaration of thought sustain him, the less he would fear the coming winter days.

He kicked a little pebble to the side of the path. Would it lie there to be scratched by a *vigneron*'s boots, roll into the gutter or be shoveled again into the soil to stay for a generation before some peasant's spade turned it over and brought it again into the light? In every village generations were born and died without once opening a book. He could find no reason why he had been singled out to be more fortunate than his cousin in these times but he had the wisdom of the past to give him fortitude whereas the peasants, even when the crops were good, thought only of the perils of tomorrow.

Yes, he, Alexandre, was mightier than Their Excellencies, he was a scholar, even if this made people avoid him. It was like drinking the wine of the great summer of a century. Only December would come and the cold, he knew every crack in the wall through which the wind whistled as if on purpose to torment him and the craving for a little hot soup that could block his thoughts and once had tempted him to snatch a roasted chestnut by bumping against a stall.

It was late, the exultation was dying that was due more to his last meal (if he could only admit it) than to the range of his imagination, and he was thankful to reach the shelter of the house where he lodged. A ragged urchin to whom he occasionally gave a crust that he really wanted to eat himself, was standing beside the door.

"Monsieur!" The boy's eyes were fixed on the scholar as if in the hope that an apple would spill out of his pocket, "Monsieur, I've been waiting for you for an hour."

"I have been away," Alexandre fumbled in the pocket of his coat but there was only a hole in the lining that he had forgotten to ask his cousin's wife to mend.

"Monsieur Guilléron sent me to ask you to come to his office at three tomorrow." The urchin looked Alexandre up and down from his battered hat to his dusty shoes. All the same, the old man would have to pay the requisition along with everyone else even if he had nothing afterwards to buy a bit of firewood. Perhaps he did not have a batz to spare but surely, if he had been in the country, he had brought back a bit of fruit with him?

"My friend, the notary, up in the Bourg?"

"Yes," the boy nodded, he had been given a coin for doing the errand but he was still not convinced that the scholar's pockets were really empty. "At three, it's important," he repeated and then, seeing that the old man had both hands clasped firmly round his stick, he ran off whistling down the road.

Guilléron. They had been schoolfellows and still greeted each other if they happened to meet but why should the notary want to see him? Had somebody complained that he had spoken incautiously about Berne? It would not matter now if he had but it was hard to still the old fears. Had he been denounced for some chance remark about the right of farmers to withhold the tithes? He had no money for a fine and how would he survive the damp cell into which they would put him, perhaps for weeks, before they even considered his case? Or could it be that someone, a foreigner perhaps, had asked the notary to recommend a tutor to teach his son French?

He brushed the dust from his stockings before entering the house so that his landlady would not reproach him for dirtying her floor but the glory of the day had gone and he wondered, almost spitefully, why his cousin had not given him just one bunch of the grapes he had helped to pick and a slice or two of bread?

It was pleasant at a time when he had usually bad news for his clients to have something favorable to announce and that to a former schoolfellow. He never saw him without a prickling of his conscience. Alexandre, the brilliant Alexandre, as they had called him in their classes, was worthy of a better position than being an itinerant tutor and he could have found him one with a landowner near Nyon if only he had not been so open an antagonist of Berne. Guilléron looked down at his desk, idly straightening the already tidy papers while he wondered if people had noticed how much he had had to retrench himself? The farmer on his own estate had paid no dues for a year and the whole property was so small that he dared not ask him for them. There was some talk of compensation at the Council but if it came, the bigger landlords would put their claims in first and meantime there was a big gap in his income. He had planned to have the tool shed mended and to buy himself a thick winter waistcoat but now these would have to wait. The most serious problem was fuel. It had doubled in price and they dared not light the painted stove that was his wife's delight. At present, and he hoped his clients would not hear about it, there was nothing to do but sit with the servants in the kitchen in the evenings.

There was a knock at the door. "Come in, Alexandre, come in," he sprang up to greet his friend so rapidly that he almost knocked the worn hat out of the scholar's hand. Alexandre had had his hair powdered for the occasion and had put on an old but respectable suit. He had been thinking of his father's advice all morning, "If you are summoned before an official, always wear your best clothes. They will take more notice of you if you are of good appearance."

"How have you been? I have not seen you since we met walking on Montbenon last April."

"Thank you, Étienne, well." Now that there was such a gap between them he wondered if he ought to use his friend's first name? "Did you have a pleasant summer?"

"Nobody in Lausanne could have had a pleasant summer with all this unrest. I have been to Cully several times and once to Nyon for various clients but with little success. The peasants will not pay their dues, we are promised compensation but after the ransom we had to pay the French for 'liberating' us, there is no money in the treasury."

"All things take time."

"If they take much longer, Lausanne, as we have known it, will cease to exist. If you could hear the stories people tell me, people who owned their carriages and even big estates and are now thinking of emigration in order to live, you would wish the old days, even if Berne was tyrannical at times, were back again. But what about yourself? I haven't seen you lately, have you been away?"

"I went to a cousin for a month to help him with the grapes. The air was good and the crop as well. The schools and my lessons have only just begun again." How could a notary, and Guilléron was said to be a successful one, understand what a month of sunshine and regular meals meant to a hungry scholar?

"I know your cousin's farm. It must be shady there in summer with the walnut trees at the side of it."

The rich silver inkstand, two pens and a smooth quire of paper belonged to the law rather than to a scholar's table. There was not a speck of dust anywhere. Only why, Alexandre wondered, had Étienne summoned him? His friend was hesitating as if unwilling to tell him of some ominous news yet what could he have done? He had written no pamphlets nor taken part in any political debate. He tried to keep calm although his hand was gripping the edge of his chair, in a moment, although he did not want his friend to perceive his anxiety, he would blurt out some stupid question.

Étienne got up slowly and unlocked a drawer with a key that seemed too small for the great cabinet of polished wood. He was deliberate in his movements because he was looking forward to seeing how his friend would take his surprising news. Could they have been schoolfellows? Alexandre looked so old. He found the packet that he had already put carefully at the top of the drawer, looked at the fresh quill that was in readiness on the table, at the long, curved rose painted on the front of another cupboard at the end of the room and down at the carpet that was showing signs of wear. "Do you remember Monsieur Duclos?" he asked.

"Duclos? Of course, but he died last June." He missed his friend, they had always found some point to discuss in the news and he avoided now, it seemed so lonely, the bench where they had sat at Montbenon.

"An estimable citizen, I am sure, you will agree."

"I enjoyed our conversations and he was as fond of walking as I am."

"An honest action brings its own reward." Étienne knew this was not true as he repeated the proverb; in his own experience honesty earned a fine more often than a prize.

"You are right." Alexandre wondered who was wearing now the summer suit of which Duclos had been so proud? He had teased him about it because the first day he had worn it they had looked up to see a squirrel on a branch that was exactly the same brown. Why had the notary fetched him to question him about a man who had been merely a chance acquaintance? Or perhaps, and the scholar felt an immense relief, there might be a relative they had not been able to trace and Étienne felt that he might know the name of the man's village.

"You helped him, I believe, in the matter of some assignats."

"Oh, those assignats! Yes, but that was years ago and I advised him to change them immediately. There was such unrest in France." Surely to give an opinion to a friend was not a breach of the law. He fumbled for his handkerchief so that Étienne would not notice that his hands were trembling.

"If he had not taken your advice, he would have lost a third of his fortune. His house and land went to some distant cousin but having no near relations he remembered you when he made his will, here in this very room, a few months before he died. He left you this."

Alexandre took the packet and could he have known it, his astonishment made up to Étienne for the chilly autumn air that was invading the unheated room. It was so heavy that he almost dropped it, he turned it over, yes, it was addressed to him in care of Monsieur Étienne Guilléron, could it be, no, of course it could not be anything so costly, what he had always longed for, a watch?

"You had better open it, here's a knife."

If he had a watch, he would not be obliged to leave for the school so early on a cold day nor worry over being late. It might cost money to keep it in order but it was somehow a scholar's right although his favorite proverb, "Keep yourself free from possessions," flashed across his mind. His hands shook, he looked for an opening where he could slit the package open although it seemed a pity to spoil such good paper, he fumbled until Étienne smiled and took it out of his hands. The notary ripped the covering away and handed a linen bag back to him. "Don't be afraid of it, Alexandre, it is not a weapon."

The bag was not the shape of a book, it was too heavy for a watch. Oh, now he knew what it was going to be, geological specimens. They were fashionable at the moment and perhaps he could sell them, in time, to buy some firewood. "It is pleasant to be remembered," he must not let Étienne see his disappointment, besides, if they were some of the scarcer rocks, they could be valuable.

"Be careful."

A *louis d'or* rolled out of the bag and bumped to the floor, another followed it, spinning along the desk, he had to pull the bag together to prevent the rest from spilling over his knees. "But it's gold, I thought it was a packet of specimens, crystal perhaps or basalt!" The stupor on the scholar's face compensated Étienne for the gloomy thoughts that had been haunting him for days. "Hadn't you better count them? And then we can tie them up again."

"They can't be mine."

"He left them to you."

"But it was because I remembered the difficulties after the Punic Wars that I advised him to trust gold and not paper."

"I doubt your friend Duclos knew anything about the

Romans but your advice saved him a lot of his fortune. Speculating in assignats ruined more than ever gained from it."

"And his heir?"

"Don't be a fool, Alexandre. The man has inherited a house worth far more than these coins. But be wise, tell nobody about the legacy or say, if you must, that a kinsman left you five *louis.*"

"I cannot take it to my lodging. I am out all day and it might be stolen."

"I think you are wise." Étienne had planned his approach carefully because he intended to look after his friend if possible. "If you will trust it to me, I will buy you a piece of land. What with the taxes and various other difficulties I know of a place I can get cheaply not far from Lausanne. There will be a small legal fee but I will keep it as low as possible."

"Land? What should I do with land?"

"It's an investment. I shall sell it for you again as soon as the times improve. You will not need to live there, a peasant is already farming it, but if you let me look after the matter, you will have a steady income, even if it is a small one, when you are ready to give up teaching. But first let us see how much you have."

A *louis d'or.* One piece would buy not only enough firewood for the winter but also a thick cloak. Three or perhaps four could get him the watch that he wanted but Étienne was right, he must think of the future. He could not resist turning a few of the coins over in his hand and he thought of Duclos and the way he had of putting his hands on his knees and saying, "The trouble with the French is that they talk too much." Then suddenly there had been battles instead of debates. It was all so puzzling, they had never even had a glass of wine together, "Why, why, did he leave this money to me?"

"Stop saying why and count it. There should be a hundred pieces. Then if you will sign this receipt, I will lock it up in my cupboard and invest it as soon as possible to your advantage."

It was golden and beautiful, a better color than the sunset because that faded and the metal was durable and hard. "Could I keep one piece," he pleaded as if he were a child, "otherwise when I wake tomorrow morning how can I believe it has happened?"

"Take five with you and celebrate your good fortune."

Duclos! The Punic Wars! His scholarship, his despised scholarship had helped him at the end. And Étienne's honesty. Why, his friend could have taken the money and never said a word to him about it. Then in a spirit of daring such as he had never felt since he had won a swimming race as a boy, he said as if his cravat were new and his waistcoat pure silk, "Étienne, after you have locked this away, may I invite you to the *Lion d'Or* for supper?"

Chapter Eleven

Winter, 1801

Amiens! It was a magic word that released the restraint of years and was for some the beginning and for others the end of hope. Mazelet knew finally that independence was not the end of poverty, the émigrés, that strangers would still occupy the houses they had left in France because they could not afford to return. Other foreigners simply waited for April when the roads would dry and they could go back to their homes after an involuntary exile. "It's not our city any longer," Laurent grumbled as he strolled along Montbenon after church on Sundays, but after the alarms and rumors of the previous summer there was a general feeling of liberation after the Peace.

They pointed him out as a foreigner, Philippe knew, but this time he was treated as a guest when he walked down the street, always carefully avoiding the market place, in a suit made from the finest dark blue cloth that the tailor could provide. He had been foolish to return, he had recognized this after his first day in Lausanne but some instinct had driven him here, some stupid, emotional feeling of which he was now ashamed, to try to obliterate the past. They talked about their Revolution to his amusement but what had they changed? There were the same cobbles with the same scratches; why, he was sure if he looked sharply enough, he could still find the head of a nail he had once dropped, flattened between two stones. The inn sign, the broad faces, the round, black buttons on the porter's coat, were identical with the ones he had left six years before. Nobody had altered but himself and with him it was the outward show, people looked enviously at his white, almost transparent linen and his silk cravat, but inwardly he was the same proud, dissatisfied youth who had fretted over the restrictions of old Guilléron's office. He was looking at these people as warily, as jealously, as the urchin he had been had looked, carrying a load of vegetables back to some household for some ignoble reward. That early mistrust would never vanish although he had now fulfilled one desire. He had walked down the Rue de Bourg and into the square through the same throngs of people who had screamed at him to get out of their way, to show them that Philippe Masson, the stranger, the exile, and their once so cursed at errand boy, could hire the whole of the *Lion d'Or* if he so pleased and buy finer horses for his coach than any they could afford. It had been the will to revenge himself that had carried him alive through those torrid Constantinople summers while his fellow clerks were dying from fever in their airless rooms. Or perhaps he had survived because he had spent so many hours on the water being rowed from one ship to another to haggle about cargoes instead of sitting at a desk. He could honestly say that he had always tried to get the best possible terms for his employers while never neglecting the opportunity to slip a *louis* or two for himself inside his own belt.

Yes, this return was the coming true of a dream but dreams had an awkward way of concealing surprises under their intangibility. He could stroll along this carefully swept street without needing a guard to walk a couple of paces behind him or concealing a knife under his sash, yet the narrowness of this bourgeois city was oppressive, he missed the urge to take risks, he despised the indifference of these solid citizens to all that was happening around them, did they think the war was over when it was merely postponed, and how they irritated him with their talk of planting apple trees or vines! Why were they so sure they would live to eat the fruit? It was a mistake not to have returned directly to France. Probably, he supposed, what he missed most was danger.

Success! Naturally it had its value but it had come too late to save his mother. She had followed her mistress to Lausanne though loyalty and suffering had been her only reward. Occasionally on a blazing day of eastern sunlight he had dreamed of the green slopes where he had wandered as a boy but within a day of his return he had known he could not remain in Vaud. The Peace would not last (he could feel this from the whirlpool of his own mind) there were too many divergencies for a settlement to be possible and neither land nor work enough for the many thousands of disbanded soldiers. It had been stupid to arrive so late in the year, it was now impossible to cross the frontier before the spring but then he would seek a new opening in some port until the truce, for that was all it was, ended in further warfare. Why, if he were lucky, he might gain a second, useless fortune. "You will win," he remembered his friend Abdul's solemn eyes looking up at him before his departure, on the last evening that he had seen the points of the fragile stars tracing a mosque of their own in gold on a dark sky, "you will win because it is the same to you whether you win or lose. At some point, you threw away your heart."

Six years, almost six lives, a filthy harbor and a constant battle of wits, he had endured them all to come back to a safe little town where the only unruly objects were the straggling vines, merely to discover that he was homesick for a striped awning and the single glass of smuggled wine from a visiting ship that Abdul brought him as soon as the evening call to prayer from the minaret was over.

Better a knife thrust than this slow stagnation. After all what was the end for any man but death?

Years later, when Sophie remembered that final Lausanne winter, she thought of it as one of the happiest moments of her life. It was bitterly cold, the prices went up rather than decreased and there were several violent storms. Yet Uncle Laurent suddenly took an interest in her and talked to her almost as if she had been his son, there were fewer scoldings and people who had formerly ignored her, asked her to their salons and their suppers.

Vaud was independent and her absent citizens hurried back to her, tutors from Russia in heavy furs, clerks from Dutch ports and families from Naples whose French was sprinkled with Italian words. It was a time of travelers' tales, each one more extraordinary than the last, and because the families came from so many different environments, some of the rules of what might and might not be permitted dissolved into a new freedom. She was too involved with it all, and also too inexperienced, to notice the discontent that preoccupied her uncle, "Listen, Sophie, revolutions begin when a man has no food in his barn and not from discussions in literary circles."

Vaguely, but it was weeks away, there would be her own journey to a new country. Sometimes she wondered how she would bear, not the perils that her friends kept talking about but the fresh impressions that she must cram into her head? It never occurred to her that she could miss Lausanne and she was enjoying these last days because they were the end of an experience. April was a long way off, in the meantime people said "Enjoy yourself" and she was taking them at their word.

"Have you no regrets at leaving?" they asked her at all the parties but her mother had taught her the correct reply. "Of course, but I want to meet my aunts and later I shall be coming back to you." Actually only three people mattered to her, Uncle Laurent in spite of his scoldings but once his son returned he would soon forget her, Henriette but she was interested in some lout of a fellow on a neighboring farm, and poor Monsieur Alexandre. He had more pupils now that there were so many English in Lausanne who knew little or no French and he had told her very gravely that he had inherited a small sum of money. He would miss her, she knew, and she would always be grateful to him for rescuing her from that hated school.

"Everything is loose and easy this year," her mother had said when she had given Sophie a dress for this particular New Year party. It was not only the clothes but the atmosphere that had changed; instead of the men playing cards in one room while the women clustered round the coffee cups in the salon, on this special evening they had all gathered together. She found herself sitting beside a man whose face seemed familiar although she could not recall having met him previously and though she never noticed clothes as a rule, his coat was so fine in texture and of so unusual a color that she wondered if he were some rich Dutch merchant who to avoid the muddy roads of the previous autumn, was wintering in Lausanne?

"The New Year will be with us in a few moments," he said, feeling, perhaps, that the silence was awkward. "I hope it will bring pleasant days for you."

"It will bring me a journey."

"A journey? Where?" It was safer to chat to a young girl, Philippe thought, than to have to watch his tongue among the bourgeois sitting round him in their old fashioned breeches and buckles. He might laugh out loud if he suddenly imagined them transferred to the East. What would that pompous gentleman sitting opposite do, for example, if he woke at midnight to see the glint of a knife behind the curtains round his bed? The girl was going to some relative's house, he supposed, five or six hours in a coach would seem a long journey to her.

"I am going to England." She could not imagine what the country would be like, she had no memory of it and if she thought of her aunts, they seemed almost twins of her mother.

"To England? You will have to cross the sea."

"My mother was born there and we are going to visit our relatives. My father was a Vaudois but he is dead."

"Do you want to travel?" Philippe looked at her in some amusement, wondering if she knew anything about its hardships? "I used to meet some English merchants in Constantinople." And a surly, self-opinionated assembly they had been! He had not trusted even their shadows.

"Constantinople?" To her it was the end of the world and she stared at him, wondering if he could be a Turk? "Are you from there or are you a Lausannois?"

"Neither, I was born in France but lived here as a boy." Again he seemed to feel that cold wind blowing through the market place, memory was stronger than courage, it was too forceful for reason to control it and for a moment he wanted to rush out to the stables, saddle a horse and ride it till he crossed over the frontier. Who was this girl? He flattered himself that he knew most of the bourgeois families by sight but if she were a widow's daughter, she probably lived with her mother quietly at home.

"Please tell me what Constantinople is like?" In Sophie's imagination it was a high walled town with turrets reflected in a lake-like harbor because she could not remember the sea.

"I wish I were a merchant and could go from country to country selling goods."

"One counting house is exactly like another," the card tables were tiresome to a man who had so often taken his life into his hands and Philippe found the girl's curiosity amusing. "I went there as a clerk and then I became a merchant in my own right." His first deal had been an illicit one and he had had to borrow money wherever he could find it to pay some essential bribes but after he had got the cargo he had sold it to a drunken trader for almost double its value. It had been the start of his fortune. "Constantinople? It is hot in summer but the alleys are funnels in winter for a knife-like wind and in both seasons people die like flies."

"Yet you must have liked it or you would not have stayed."

Liked it? Yes, he supposed he had or he would have shipped in some vessel to another port. Six years, six lives, endless fevers, a stab that had merely caught his shoulder, the plot to take the place of a fellow clerk so that he would always be the first to board some ship stinking of bilge water and filth on the chance of winning an additional *louis* to add to the gradually accumulating hoard that he had deposited with a merchant of his acquaintance, all were a part of the only method he had found to ease the hatred and desolation of his childhood. He had a fanatical contempt for danger because he possessed, it seemed, no ties to life. Some instinct had warned him to learn Turkish so as not to rely upon interpreters and in that way he had found Abdul, the only friendship of his youth. They could meet each other easily because they must always be strangers, coming from different worlds yet each holding the same counters, hardship, cold, hunger and ambition, to play for or against existence. "We cannot determine our fate," Abdul's white sleeve would billow above the handle of the coffee cup that was all the drinking that his

young Lausannois of her own age in the room, she had contrived to sit next that questionable foreign merchant. People gossiped about him, they said he was the son of an exiled French marquis and had had to leave the city earlier because of being implicated in a royalist plot, but that was nonsense. He had once been a beggar boy for whom Laurent had found work. Yet now he was occupying the best rooms at the *Lion d'Or* and was received by the best circles in the city. It showed what money could do for a man if he made it. Ought she to get up and take Sophie away? No, nothing could happen to the girl, sitting in the same room as herself, if on a different side of it. It was better to let things be than to risk a stormy scene, "I can look after myself," when the party was over. Oh, her daughter had joined the group that was handing round the New Year cakes. She was glad now that she had not interrupted the conversation.

"So you are leaving us in the spring, Madame Perrin?"

"Yes, it is almost fifteen years since I saw my sisters and Mrs. Peterson has invited me to accompany her." Everyone in the room knew that she had no money otherwise to pay for the journey but it seemed more dignified to pretend that she was accompanying her employer as a friend.

"But you are coming back to us, I hope?" It was sheer politeness because Monsieur Guilléron saw her perhaps once a year and could not care what happened to the poor relatives of his best client but it was pleasant to sit among these grave, intelligent people after listening for days to Mrs. Peterson's dreary grumbles. The woman hated everything and yet had not known a single anxiety since the day she was born. What would life be like when she finally rejoined her sisters? Would it involve the feelings of being "foreign" again or would there be some hazy early remembrance to help her under the new conditions? No matter how she had tried, they had never accepted her here although she might have stayed if the tie to her sisters, her own real family, was not drawing her back. Besides, there was Sophie. The child would have no opportunities as long as she remained here. Yet how she would miss Laurent! He was happier and less tired now that Antoine was coming back to join him, with praise from the merchant in whose office he had worked and business to transact for him here. Would she, herself, return? Could she, whatever her memories, face a second change after being reunited with her sisters? It might depend on Sophie but surely the girl was young enough to settle into a new home? How foolish she was! This was real coffee and they were offering her a second cup, young Madame Guilléron was smiling at her, even her daughter was laughing with a group of young companions at the end of the room. It was like the New Year evenings with her parents before she had known Daniel or had ever imagined that life could be unsheltered and lonely.

The turn of the year, she hoped a new and pleasant life was waiting for them all because during the whole evening she had not heard a quarrelsome word and how strange but comforting it was that nobody had mentioned either liberty or Berne.

Chapter Twelve

May, 1802

May was the month when the sky and the lake were the same blue and the hills a line of gray in the distance. A boat with a patch of white at its stern pulled out from the sandy shore. Madame Perrin adjusted her shawl, its texture was the only thing that seemed familiar because even the gate that she had opened and shut for so many years seemed without substance, the description of a doorway in some stranger's village, vivid to him because he remembered it but without meaning to the listener. She was thankful that she had arranged to say goodbye to her brother-in-law at his home instead of hurriedly in the middle of an excited crowd the following day. The packing for Mrs. Peterson was finished, she hoped that the new bonnets were in a stout enough box, that the cordial was safely on top of the traveling basket and that Sophie would master her exuberance for once and behave sedately as they drove away. She was sad herself. She knew she would never see Laurent again no matter what excuses they might make to each other nor this house that had been her refuge during the past years whenever she had been able to escape for an hour from her exacting mistress. Even as she looked up at the line of lime trees along the side of the garden she thought of August and of how much she enjoyed picking the flowers for a tisane before she remembered that she would not be here even to see the buds open. A last time, these were words, words, floating on the surface of her mind, underneath; however much she felt the parting at this immediate moment, there was an overmastering desire to return to her sisters and a place where she was rightfully at home. Only she would miss Laurent. His present affection had grown so slowly out of his early, vexed toleration of her that it was truly a triumph. She need not grieve, he would soon have his son. According to his last letter, Antoine must have already sailed to Holland and once he had finished some business there, would be on his way home. The growth of events made her feel as if destiny really was calculated in advance even if she had sometimes misunderstood the events as they happened.

"This is a sad day for both of us," Laurent came down the path to meet her, "however, although I do not envy you your traveling companions, the Petersons are rich and will put up at the best inns."

"I shall miss you as well." She would never regret the mountains of which she was afraid but she knew she would often turn to make some comment to Laurent, forgetting the seas and leagues of land that would separate them once she got home. He needed her, she knew, it was harder for him than for many of his fellow Vaudois to face the new and unwelcome changes because he had always disliked any variation in his habits. If Marthe were a minute late in bringing in the soup, it upset him for the whole evening.

"It will be just for a year, I hope." Both of them were aware that it was doubtful if she would return but to pretend that she was merely going for a visit made the parting easier.

"I wish I could join the Petersons outside Lausanne tomorrow. Then we could dine together, I should assume that you were off to visit your cousin at Morges and when I left, I would wave and say, 'Till our meeting next Sunday.'" Her favorite white roses would flower, it would be Marthe who would fill the old basket with lime blossoms, gradually the summer heat would fade into the autumn golds of leaves and straw and wind. It seemed silly to repeat it again but what else could she say? "I shall miss you more than Lausanne, Laurent, I wish you were coming with us."

"I was angry when Daniel married you and brought you here. A young woman needs to be reasonably near her own family. But afterwards I was glad. You gave him happiness as long as he was alive. Later, you have given me companionship."

"Antoine should be back by July."

"He will have changed. Now he is a merchant in his own right. Not the boy I fed with apples and scolded."

"You need not be afraid." She knew from her own experience that even six years in a foreign country would not have altered him. "You will find him more serious but so happy to come home."

"I wish I could have helped you more." It had been a shock to Laurent's pride to have his sister-in-law working for the Petersons. "But as I told you, once the peasants broke away from Berne, the taxes rose and money depreciated. Liberty may be a fine word but it's a costly luxury."

Yet it gave us an identity, Madame Perrin checked the words just in time before uttering them. At that moment she was one with her daughter, the white and green cockade was better than a golden *louis*. "You have helped me so much," she tried to bring the conversation back to a more personal level, "remember I have had Sophie and your friendship."

Far off, very far off, she could see the mountains that had been the cause of her only quarrel with Daniel. They had represented force to him and some kind of happiness that she could not understand. She had not realized this at the time but now whenever she thought about him, her real grief was that he had had to spend so many years away from the land he loved. "If they could only find a herb against our fevers."

"And against our age." She saw in Laurent's eyes that he knew they would never see each other again. Then, as if to excuse the sudden flash of knowledge that had passed between them, he added, "I never supposed that I should miss Antoine so much."

Sophie paused to look down at the lake, a puff of wind was wrinkling its flat surface but it was too early in the season otherwise for many boats to be out although two fishermen were patching a sail that was spread out on the shingle down by the harbor. She had been sent on an errand and was anxious not to return too soon lest she disturb her mother's leave-taking. Besides, the house oppressed her, it seemed so dark, so still, in spite of Uncle Laurent's new friendliness and of his having invited her to spend the last few days with him before the journey.

Would she be more free or less free when she got to England? She could not imagine her aunts; "My sisters were different," her mother had always said, "I was the adventurous one. You will have more liberty in some ways but you won't be able to run around in overalls in the summer, herding goats." Perhaps they would expect her to sit indoors all day and only speak if she were asked a question? She was tired of trying to imagine it or of thinking about the seasons, the good days were brief and the ones when the *bise* cracked round the corners desolate and long. She tramped on again so impatiently that she almost bumped into a figure hurrying in the opposite direction. *"Bonjour,* mademoiselle," the voice was familiar and she glanced up to see the young merchant who had sat next to her at the New Year party, sweeping off his hat. "Daydreaming or puzzled?" he inquired in a mocking tone that annoyed her. She must answer a salutation from an acquaintance, her mother had trained her, but then walk on immediately towards her destination. Yet she had often thought about Philippe and though she had seen him once at another party, he had been sitting on the opposite side of the room and, apart from a polite greeting, they had not talked. "I was wondering what my new home would be like. We are leaving for England tomorrow."

"It's early in the season but the inns will be less crowded. I am going to France myself next week. It's natural to dream but I feared that you were going to bump into that wall. Are you a little afraid of meeting your relatives?"

"No, I want to see them but I thought the Liberation was going to be like opening the gate into a field where they used to say 'No trespassing.' We should be able to follow our natures. My cousin ran away because he did not want to be a notary's clerk, I should like to enter a counting house. It cannot be more difficult to enter items of cargo in a ledger than to stack jars of dusty herbs into a cupboard."

"Marry a sea captain and persuade him to take you with him on his journeys."

"Never!" By now Sophie was really indignant. "Why did we speak of Liberation and light bonfires if conditions are always going to be exactly the same?"

"Not quite the same."

"I want to depend on myself and not be at the mercy of chance as my mother has been all these years." Sophie forgot that she was standing in a road and not sitting demurely in a salon but it seemed of utmost importance to make her position clear to the young merchant.

"We always want life to change." Philippe knew now why the girl had a shadowy attraction for him. It was the same loyalty that his mother had felt for her most unworthy mistress whereas the Perrin child felt it for an idea and had, as well, something of his own restless curiosity. "Yet if it does, there is always the old current underneath. People talk about revolution but we all mean something different by the word."

"Then is there never to be freedom?"

"Yes, when we have more knowledge." He had read the philosophers and they might have found an answer for themselves but not as yet for a man who had been born restless and stamped by despair. "There are moments," but this he knew Sophie was too inexperienced to understand, "you were happy at the New Year party, you will find your journey interesting and there will be much to learn when you get to your new home. I am leaving as well next week for France." The peace would not last and he must establish himself securely in some port before hostilities began. "We are wanderers in a world that does not understand us but remember, we see and feel more than those who have roots. I shall hear of you through my agent in London and perhaps we shall meet again in some port if you take my advice and marry a captain. You must take the moments, remember summer and forget the *bise*." He walked on so swiftly that he was round the corner before Sophie realized that he had gone.

Monsieur Alexandre stretched himself and pulled the covers almost over his ears. This was the chief privilege that affluence had brought him, he could stay in bed until seven o'clock instead of getting up at six. His toes were warm, his nightcap kept out the drafts and he forgot for an instant that he would have to hurry if he wanted to see Sophie leave. Would it not be better to remember her waving to him from the threshold of her uncle's house where he had seen her last than to watch the coach rumbling over the cobbles toward a foreign land?

The boxes of that odious Mrs. Peterson would be piled so high against the windows that he might not even get a glimpse of the girl as she left. No, this was an excuse, a mere shrinking from the cold, and he sprang out of bed, thankful that there was plenty of light coming into the room when he threw open the shutters so that he did not have to fumble with a tinder-box and candle. It might be May but his hands and feet grew chilly while he dressed. He put on a waistcoat that he had had lined with mountain wool and drew over it his thin Sunday coat. "Your soup is ready," Madame Reymond called from outside the door. She looked after him (and he liked to roll the words round his tongue) not as if he were a distant relative but an ambassador. "There is no time," the stairs creaked as he walked slowly down them and he could hear the carts already rumbling past on their way to the market.

"Of course there is time. I didn't get up early to make that soup for nothing. You must have something hot before you go out. Even if it is spring, there's still a nip in the air and besides I know what those drivers are like. They load the carriage, then they turn everything out and put the boxes back another way although it is all the same at the end. Your friends will be lucky if they start by eight o'clock." She blocked the doorway so that he had to sit down and it was comforting to feel the hot liquid sliding down his throat in spite of his anxiety. He kept taking one sip after the other until the bowl was empty and he felt really awake. After all, what chance would he have to speak to Sophie? There was nothing more he could say and all he could hope for was a final, torturing glimpse of her.

"They'll be back." Was Madame Reymond looking at him with pity or amusement? "After fifteen years here, how can they settle in England? I understand Madame Perrin. She'll never get her inheritance unless she goes to London to claim it. It's easy enough for those sisters to pretend she is dead. Wait and see. Once she has the money she will come back here. You said yourself it ought to be enough to buy them a little house. As for the daughter, a journey at her age is the same as if somebody had given her a painted ribbon."

A painted ribbon. It was the way that his life seemed to unroll in front of him as he walked down the street. He even looked round uneasily in case he had said the words aloud. Would it matter if he had? The day was early and there were few people as yet on the roads. He had always had the sun, the water and his staff that was actually a vine stock for his companions; slights were almost part of a teacher's pay, but he had had the glory of learning to sustain him and he had lived to see the independence of Lausanne. He had met Duclos and that lucky accident had brought him wealth (even though his fellow citizens would laugh at him for using such a word to describe his little fortune) and the terrifying fear that he would finish his life as a pensioner at some asylum had left him. Yet Sophie was going away and with her went summer. Why was she so willful? Surely she could have persuaded her mother to leave her in her uncle's charge? She had forgotten his lessons in the excitement of the journey, their conviction that freedom was greater than a title. *She will come back.* Oh, he was as certain of her return as he was that eventually the neediest peasant would add his voice to the discussion of the laws. Only by then he might be an old man, asking no more than a bowl of soup, the seat next the stove in winter or a bench in summer under a shady tree. He hoped his memories would not fly away as the birds did before the first frosts, he wanted to keep them all, Neptune in some festival, rising from the lake, the silver drops from his beard pitting the water like a flock of little moor hens, those heaps of grass at his cousin's farm with a rake lying across them, Sophie's face when he had spoken to her of liberty. She would come back, she must come back, he was almost anxious for her to go so that he could start hoping for her return. Perhaps it was just a wish? He had wanted everything but gold and gold ironically had been the one gift the gods had given him. "Let it be soon," he mumbled to himself, suppose death forgot him in the turbulence of the times and he became a muttering, rheumatic carcass bereft of feeling and mind, so that when the coach (it must bring Sophie back) clattered over the stones again, he was too stiff to rise and greet her.

"Reviens!" A gentleman in a coat that was slightly too long and the brown that was unfashionable this season, handed Mrs. Peterson into her carriage.

"Promise to come back. How can we stage a New Year play without you?" Most of the English still left in Lausanne had assembled opposite the inn.

"Otherwise I shall ride back to England before my studies are finished and wait on you at your home."

Who was that fool? Sophie looked in the direction of the voice. It might be the idiot in a dove colored cravat when all the others were wearing white ones or that stranger whom she did not recognize in the back row. They all disliked Mrs. Peterson but they loved her husband's guineas. A stable boy grinned as a feather in the lady's elaborate bonnet caught against the door and almost broke.

"You have the basket, Sophie?"

Of course she had the basket but how was she going to endure the journey? She had promised a dozen times she would behave but they were going to pass meadows and apple trees, lakes and mountains, whose names she knew from songs and tales and what would she see of them, sitting backwards in the coach with Mrs. Peterson's querulous face in front of her and some great hamper obscuring even a crack of the tiny window? How could she bear to watch her mother being treated as if she were a serving woman and she supposed she would be kept busy taking messages herself, wherever they stopped. "Liberty and Equality," she whispered to herself, "all of us are equal," even if the words brought back Uncle Laurent's teasing voice, "The Bernois as well, of course."

"A deserter! Proclaim her a deserter." It was the man in the cravat but was he smiling or being as ironical as the messenger in a stupid play that she had had to watch at Christmas? Mrs. Peterson leaned forward and waved to them all. Two servants carried out the last bundles while Sophie waited for her turn to mount. She seemed by now to have been standing there for hours. Her mother had been wise to insist upon their making their own farewells the previous day so as not to disturb Mrs. Peterson's own leave-taking from her friends. The coachman looked round, a boy tightened a strap.

"Sophie!"

Now she would be blamed for daydreaming again. She squeezed her way through the ostlers but nobody offered to help her clamber up into the carriage. Her mother motioned her to sit on a hard, narrow seat and, of course, just as she had supposed, the biggest of the Peterson hampers cut off all but a narrow slit of the window. If only she had been a boy she could have ridden behind Mr. Peterson. He had hired a horse for the first stages of the journey and looked happy for the first time since his arrival; besides, he seemed so much more at ease in his riding coat than bulging out of the flowered waistcoat that he had to wear at *Le Cercle*.

It was unfair, all life was unfair if one were a Sophie and not an Antoine or a Philippe. She pulled the basket gently a scrap further from the window while her companions were talking and waving, otherwise a dark partition would separate her from seeing even the dust of that revolutionary France of which she had heard so much.

"Au revoir, chère madame."

"Reviens! Reviens!"

"I believe they will really miss me." Mrs. Peterson leaned forward to wave at the same time that the driver cracked his whip. The carriage jolted forward and she fell back against Madame Perrin. "My ribs! Oh, my ribs! They will be cracked before we get to Yverdon."

"A few drops of cordial! Sophie, the basket!"

The voices rose to such a din that no words were audible. A hamper almost fell on Sophie's head and her mother began to rearrange the cushions that had been dislodged by their precipitate start. They turned into the square, she felt inside her pocket for the faded, green cockade that Monsieur Alexandre had once given her. He had told her that he would stand beside the church and in defiance of all authority she pushed the hamper further aside and leaned forward to look out of the window. Alexandre was waiting just as he had promised, with a new, white cravat tucked inside his Sunday coat. *Adieu!* He could not hear her voice because of the grinding of the wheels upon the stones. *Adieu!* She shouted a second time and waved. He waved back and she knew that he had seen her. "Have you forgotten yourself?" Madame Perrin scolded, pushing the hamper back in its original position. Now for a whole long day she would face its wicker stems instead of a new landscape. Yet for a moment she had seen not only her faithful if often puzzling tutor but the hills and two familiar walnut trees behind a garden wall. It might be, the thought was surprising rather than sad, that she would never return. The parting came easily, it seemed as ordinary an event as a flock of birds rising daily at their appointed time above the lake. Unlike the others, she needed no farewells, she had her inheritance no matter where her destiny might lead her, the white and the green, the snowflakes and the vines, that were the colors and the emblems of Vaud.